COUNTRY
CHRISTMAS

A Comptons Novella

Fiona Walker

Cover design by: Foof

For Trischa, with love and tinsel.

PART ONE

T here were stirrings of seasonal insurgence in the Bardswolds village of Compton Magna this Christmas. The Chair of the Parish Council, who traditionally organised the carol singing, was away visiting a new granddaughter. Into the fold stepped primary school head Auriol Bullock and local vicar Hilary Jolley.

The pairing led to a partisan clash.

Culture-loving Auriol, who had directed the village's recent outdoor production of Mamma Mia, was eager to create a fiesta-like celebration of world music: '*Vive Le vent. Feliz Navidad, Mary's Boy Child, Last Christmas!*'

On God's side, the Reverend Hilary Jolley preferred to recreate a traditional nativity procession harking the herald angels, complete with small children, sheep and a donkey.

The only thing on which Auriol and Hilary agreed was that the "donkey" which had stolen everyone's hearts at last summer's musical was a much-needed crowd-puller. 'We have the fake fur ears readymade!'

The "donkey" disagreed. Fearing he was being

typecast, Shetland Pony Coll flatly refused to have anything to do with it. When the Reverend Jolley - who claimed to have a St Francis-like way with animals - tried a carrot and stick approach, Coll ate the carrot and then showed what he thought of the stick. It was only the swift intervention of Coll's owner Petra that prevented the vicar from joining their Maker.

'We can't force him into it!' She defended her indignant, hairy charge. 'He's entirely the wrong species.'

'She'll be accusing us of cultural approbation next,' muttered Auriol, who found romance writer Petra Gunn frustratingly soppy and woke. The Reverend was still too winded to comment.

There was nothing for it, they agreed; a real donkey must be found.

Eager to make up for Coll's teeth marks on hallowed flesh, Petra agreed to take personal responsibility, vowing: 'and if I can't find one, I will be the back end in a fancy-dress suit. That's a promise!'

*

'We'll go out soon,' Gill promised her tall, roman-nosed gelding as she posted more slices of hay over his stable's half-door at guilty speed, rewarding his wickers of excitement with a hurried pat.

When her husband and three daughters had all ridden, the little yard behind the family's cottage would have a face over every glowing door and tinsel strung along the gutters this close to

Christmas. But one by one they'd lost interest, and Gill Walcote was the family's last horseman standing, her rangy bay its solitary herd member. Both were often bored and lonely.

Gill was not having the easiest festive season. Its comforts and joys had lost some of their glow in recent years: her sociable teenagers were always out, her own parents no longer alive, and she was unromantically wedded to her work as well as to taciturn vet Paul Wish, with whom she ran their busy equine practice.

This year, with one young colleague sidelined by a broken ankle, another by a family crisis, the Walcote-Wishes had been forced to cancel a much-anticipated trip to visit Paul's family in New Zealand. Instead, the couple were on call throughout Christmas.

Paul was in a constant bad temper as a result, their daughters also monstrously disappointed. The youngest two had been moping around the house with long faces since school term ended; the oldest had announced she was now spending Christmas with her boyfriend's family in Devon.

To top it all, Great Aunt Evelyn had got wind of the change and invited herself to stay for Christmas week, eager to get away from her retirement home's relentless infantile jollity, her arrival imminent. The last of Gill's father's generation, 'Aunt Evil' was legend for her gin-soaked self-absorption.

Paul was so furious with his wife for agreeing he was now barely speaking to her, as though

Gill was personally trying to ruin his Christmas. The couple had weathered many tough patches in their twenty-five-year marriage, but this one felt particularly testing. So much so that when her close friend Petra Gunn dropped round with her big brown eyes and a box of iced gingerbread stars, the normally trap-tight, Keep-Calm-and-Carry-On Gill confided: 'The atmosphere is toxic. Paul's been sleeping in the spare room all week.'

'I wish Charlie kipped in ours,' Petra sighed enviously, 'I've no hope of hearing Santa's sleigh bells over his snoring.' She was too preoccupied to offer more than a sympathetic hug. Her Shetland Coll had almost killed the vicar on a trial run of that week's carol-singing procession, she explained. 'I promised I'd help find a replacement, but Silver Hooves Sanctuary said 'no' to borrowing one of theirs. Can you believe it? My kids have been sponsoring Yankee and Doodle for a decade! I have just forty-eight hours. You must know somebody?'

Lying awake that night, hearing the long-case clock strike one downstairs, Gill sensed the universe was trying to tell her something.

There was only one person she knew locally guaranteed to be in a position to help: Robbie Marlborough kept a small donkey herd at his rare breeds farm in Broad Compton, bred by his mother, Betty.

But Bobby and Gill hadn't spoken for almost forty years.

Not since she'd broken off their engagement.

Her greatest mistake, she would realise later, was revealing this detail to Petra.

*

Petra adored Christmas, especially its redemptive kindness, on which she joyfully feasted to balance out the commercial excess, like Berocca offsetting Bloody Marys. When Gill revealed a jaw-dropping secret from her past, she took it as a sign that peace on earth - at least in this small fold of the Bardswolds - depended upon her gentle handling. But the need for a donkey overrode everything.

Robbie Marlborough's number was easy enough to find; his rare breed farm even had a website, quaintly old-fashioned with pictures of Brecon Buff geese, saddleback pigs and a creamy stone farmhouse of such bucolic splendour that Petra filed it for future use as a setting for one of her steamy bodice-rippers.

A deep, smoky voice answered her call, 'Broad Compton Farm.'

Petra gave her best creamy charm in return: 'Hi Robbie, my name's Petra Gunn. I have a big favour to _'

'This is Lindy, Bob's wife. And if you want a turkey, love, forget it. We closed the Slate Blues and Norfolk Blacks order book in September.'

Petra explained her urgent quest for a donkey.

'Not from us,' Lindy Marlborough's reply came with a blast of disbelieving laughter. 'This is our busiest time of year.'

'Perhaps if I could pop up to see you and have a

chat – '

Another incredulous laugh interrupted her.

'We've no time to rustle up Eeyore for some yummy mummies down in Compton Magna.' There was a hint of a far-flung accent in the Bardswolds' burr.

Petra started explaining that she was very happy to collect and return the donkey when she realised she was talking to herself; Robbie's wife had rung off.

'How rude!'

It might have been wise to leave it there and move straight to Plan B, which involved a hastily adapted cow costume from last year's Compton Players' production of Jack and the Beanstalk and Petra bending over to walk two steps behind her unwitting husband.

But as well as being a tenacious soul, Petra was an old-fashioned romantic who had carved out a career as a historic novelist by finding stories buried as deep as fossils in stonier faces than Gill's. Her friend needed cheering up. The vet's regretful mention of a broken engagement and 'best you talk to him' had been Petra's cue, a jingle bell ding-donging merrily on high to tell her that this Christmas, she must unwrap the past.

Besides, there was no way she was being the back end of a donkey.

Scrolling her phone, she found a braying GIF from Shrek to send Gill and hurriedly composed a message beneath it.

*

'You are a darling, darling, darling girl for taking me in, Gill! Look at you, you've gone grey! *So* brave. I'm eighty-three and still a natural blonde. I've brought my own reading light, foot-spa, electric blanket and gang socket.'

Once a jet-setting fashionista, Aunt Evil still cut a dash in a lilac velour hooded tracksuit with on-trend air trainers. To accessorise the sporty look, she carried a hydro-flask everywhere, which Gill suspected contained vodka lime soda. She'd arrived with a bulging vintage five-piece Pierre Cardin luggage set, two laundry bags of fleece blankets, several dry cleaner suit carriers and a case of Hendrick's gin. The family was quietly worried she might never leave.

Contrary to Walcote family legend, Evelyn hadn't been nicknamed 'Aunt Evil' because she was demonic, although her lonely later years had lent her a devil-may-care determination.

She was the last survivor of three wartime siblings 'Vile' 'Heinous' and 'Evil', of which Gill's father, Henry 'Heinous' Walcote, had been the middle child.

Gill's aunts had shown scant interest in her childhood, visiting only sporadically and rarely remembering birthdays, wrapped up in worlds in which children played little part. Henry's older sister Violet had never married, devoted to her animals and the church, whereas Evelyn's racy marriage to handsome diplomat Ralph had kept her largely overseas.

The only exception had been a short run in the late nineteen-seventies and early eighties when, in extremis, both Violet and Evelyn had been drawn to Henry Walcote's secure homelife, its ever-ready spare bedrooms, big meals, stiff gins and pet-friendly welcome. By then in her late teens, Gill had grown fond of these two strident, fiercely independent women.

And it was during this era that the nicknames 'Aunt Vile' and 'Aunt Evil' had been conjured for charades and crackers jokes, an indomitable double-act.

'Still married to that grumpy little Kiwi, then?' Evelyn whispered after Paul had reluctantly popped out from his study for the briefest on-off smile of a greeting. 'Proved us wrong there. Vile and I were convinced it wouldn't last.'

'Our marriage?' Gil was shocked, her private fears well hidden.

'His hair! You're far too conservative for divorce, which quite ruins one's social life, take it from me. Now fix me a stiff drink while I go to the vin.'

Having shown her to the downstairs loo, Gill headed to the kitchen to fix her aunt a dilute gin and check her phone. A message from Petra made her inadvertently splash in three fingers of Tanqueray.

Need your help to get my hands on Robbie Marlborough's ass! x

*

Petra read Gill's *No!* reply with frustration.

She needed reinforcements.

Urgent Bags alert: Ladies, advice, please! She typed and sent it as a DM to local farmer's daughter Mo and trendy young mum Bridge so that Gill wouldn't see it.

The four friends made up a quartet of village riding chums known as The Saddle Bags. United by a love of horses and gossip, they were guaranteed to rally around at times of need; their motto was 'what's said in the saddle stays in the saddle'.

But the Bags hadn't met up in over a week. Dark, frosty mornings and hectic home lives made it tricky for the busy working mothers to ride together at this time of year. Petra had four children home for the hols; Gill had her short-staffed clinic; school secretary Bridge had her Polish in-laws visiting; and smallholder Mo was being kept busy by her family's Christmas tree plantation. When not sharing secrets on horseback, the foursome relied upon WhatsApp to stay in touch.

Petra had always been the most loquacious messenger, punctuating hours waiting for inspiration in her 'Plotting Shed' with a lot of thumb twiddling and emojis. This meant the others were accustomed to ignoring her.

It took two more messages, three GIFs and a screaming emoji to get any response. That came from Bridge, who being under thirty-five, primarily communicated in acronyms: *WTF?*

By contrast, Petra used complex sentences with

punctuation, adjectives, exaggeration and artistic license to explain that Gill's former fiancé was the only one who could save her from the back end of a panto donkey costume. Or, more accurately, a cow costume with Coll's *Mamma Mia* ears sewn on.

Two more *WTF*, an *LMAO*, *STFU* and *IYKYK* later, Bridge seemed to agree that Petra shouldn't let Gill's non-cooperation or Robbie Marlborough's wife stop her quest for a live-action donkey.

At least, that's how Petra interpreted it.

*

Gill still had Robbie's engagement ring. She'd always felt bad about keeping it, but he'd never asked for it back, and the awkwardness of time passing had made offering it an impossibility. The cushion-cut emerald that had belonged to his grandmother lived in the bottom of her jewellery box, alongside her teenage pearls and a hideous cameo brooch she'd been given for her eighteenth.

Preparing for bed that night, dropping her earrings into one of the top trays, she reached in and took out the ring, amazed that it had once fitted snugly on her fourth finger, whereas now it barely slid to the first knuckle. Gill wore the wedding and engagement rings from Paul on a chain around her neck nowadays – veterinary work made it impractical to wear them on her hands – and they no longer fitted either. Perhaps she'd outgrown him too, she worried?

The arrival of Aunt Evil this evening meant they were once again sharing the same bedroom, although it was also the reason she couldn't look forward to star-fishing sleeplessly beneath the duvet with the dogs as footwarmers.

Paul was already in bed, Kindle screen illuminating his glower as he pretended to read so they didn't have to talk. Its light went out the moment she climbed in beside him, the wall of his back turning to face her. She retaliated with hers. It's how they functioned these days, mirror-miming through a silent war of attrition. Did all marriages come to this, she wondered? From memory, her parents had barely spoken from the late eighties, and they'd rubbed along well enough.

Having been more outspoken and emotional in her youth, Gill knew she had come to resemble them, stiff-upper-lip jollity papering the cracks, her husband's testiness rarely granted more attention than a faulty washing machine or car that wouldn't start every time.

Evelyn was right to say Gill was far too conservative for divorce, she acknowledged. The dramatic end to her aunt's marriage had scandalised the family, not least the tragedy of Ralph dropping dead as soon as their decree absolute was granted.

Yet here they were back-to-back in bed, she and Paul, two unhappy book ends propping up volumes of unspoken resentment.

Christmas had once brought a degree of armistice, a drunken nostalgia, but that felt a long way off this year. She hugged her horse more than her husband. Paul treated the practice receptionists far more warmly than he did her. There was one he regularly messaged out of hours, but Gill refused to let her mind work that worry bead.

On her bedside table, her phone screen lit up with a late-night message from Petra, who paid little heed to polite social curfews, especially when she and Charlie had been on the Gluhwein.

Beneath *Need your help to get my hands on Robbie Marlborough's ass!* Petra had sent an Eeyore GIF and written *Please?*

Gill felt Paul's weight shift behind her, wondering with a heart-skip of hope if he monitored her messaging as jealously as she did his.

No. She sent an angry face emoji before quickly deleting the thread, glancing guiltily over her shoulder at her husband. But he was already asleep, earplugs in.

*

Petra couldn't understand Gill's attitude at all. This was a donkey crisis!

Yet Gill had no beneficent Christmas spirit this year, it seemed, even when Petra called round to plead in person the following day, a Compton Farm Shop cinnamon cappuccino in each hand and a packet of organic Florentines clenched in her smile. 'Please come to Broad Compton Farm with me!'

'I can't,' Gill told her emphatically, then glanced up at the ceiling, lowering her voice. 'I have my elderly aunt staying. Bit of a diva, doesn't get up before midday, dipso tendencies.'

'Bring her too!' Petra sensed a kindred spirit.

'We'll grab lunch somewhere.'

'Absolutely not.' The whisper grew more strident. 'There's a jolly good reason Robbie Marlborough and I haven't spoken in all these years, so please keep me out of this. Besides, I'm far too busy to do your donkey work.'

'Haha, very funny! Surely you can spare half an hour?'

Gill remained intransigent. 'I've been belting around the Bardswolds since first light doing flexion tests on Christmas gift horses. Now I have my daughters and aunt to rally, food to prep, horse to exercise, dogs to walk and gifts to wrap. Paul's covering the clinic this afternoon, but that's no guarantee I won't be up to my elbows with an emergency colic at the drop of a Santa hat. Thank you for the coffee, but I'm passing on the ass.'

Petra, who had never seen her so uptight, guessed things between her and Paul must be even worse than she thought.

She went alone, snaking up the hill to the highest of the Compton villages, its community scattered along an escarpment overlooking the Vale of Evesham.

Turning into the rare breed farm's main entrance, Petra found herself joining a convoy of cars heading towards a thatched wooden barn with fairy lights looped along its eaves. Beyond it, she caught tantalising glimpses of the beautiful Cotswold farmhouse through the hedgerow, along with a small, railed paddock in which long ears twitched. *Donkeys!*

She paused by a gateway to admire the sight. There were at least ten of them, brown, grey and shaggy white beauties, straight out of a Christmas card.

A horn beeped, and Petra glanced into her rearview mirror, surprised by the length of the line of cars behind her as well as in front.

It was only as she drew closer to the barn that she spotted a sign reading *PRE ORDER COLLECTION 11 am - 5 pm TODAY ONLY* and realised she was in the queue to pick up one of the farm's hand-reared rare-breed turkeys and geese. It was impossible to turn around. She'd have to brazen it out.

A tall, wild-haired woman in high viz directing traffic to park.

'Put it OVER THERE, love!' she bawled at Petra in a tone that was more Brian Blessed than Beyonce, and Petra identified Lindy Marlborough with a nervous nod. At least six feet with model cheekbones and Atlas shoulders, she was Amazonian. So was Gill, come to that, but somehow less scary.

Petra hurried into the barn behind a couple in matching his-and-hers shooting coats and loitered to one side to get the lie of the land. The shooting coat couple grumbled that it was ridiculous to make everyone pick up their birds on the same day. 'But we wouldn't go anywhere else, would you? Family have been eating Marlborough birds every Chrimbo for generations.'

They were in a wooden-raftered anteroom with displays of Christmas wreaths and condiments for sale on an enormous central table. In a dividing Yorkshire board wall was a hatch at which a tall man was checking names against a list before calling back to an unseen helper to fetch the prepared bird.

This had to be Robbie Marlborough, Petra realised with an involuntary spike of excitement. Gill's ex-fiancé.

Even dressed in a white coat and hat – and was that a hairnet? - he was startlingly attractive, Daniel Craig with a side-order of Hugh Jackman. He'd be perfect cast as a battle-worn general in her new Napoleonic war series, Petra decided idly.

She was so enthralled imagining his storyline that she found herself at the front of the queue without a plan.

'Name?'

She thought fast. No, totally blank. *C'mon you're a novelist!* 'Gill Walcote!'

He looked up in surprise. Then came a lovely, intense, green-eyed smile. 'I knew a Gill Walcote. You're not her.'

'Sorry! I mean, I'm here *for* my friend Gill Walcote!'

He glanced past her shoulder as though half-expecting her to be in the anteroom too. Was it her imagination, or were those eyes looking sadder, deeper, more sea green?

'Equine vet, early fifties,' she knocked a few years off. 'Looks like Cate Blanchet.' That was pushing it.

Visibly flustered, he looked down at his clipboard. 'There's no Walcote listed here. What type of bird did she order?'

'Did I say she ordered a bird? Sorry! No, she just asked me to pick up one of these!' She reached round for a pine code wreath with one hand, then grabbed an ivy one in the other, 'and this. And three of these,' she lined up a trio of chutneys, 'Oh, and Mistletoe! She *definitely* needs this. That poor darling deserves all the kisses she can handle.'

'How d'you mean?'

She dropped her voice, 'I've already said too much. But while I'm here, can I talk to you about donkeys?'

He looked dumbfounded.

'It's alright, I *know*,' she reassured him quickly, hoping a long-ago engagement wouldn't be an impediment. 'Gill told me.'

'WHAT'S the flaming HOLD UP?' boomed Brian Blessed from the barn door, the exotic accent thickening. 'I'm running out of PARKING SPACES here, BOB!'

Robbie Marlborough smiled at Petra apologetically, taking her cash. Then he muttered urgently, 'I'll be in the pub later. Meet me there.'

Petra was back out in the car park before it occurred to her she hadn't asked which pub, but she felt victorious nonetheless, certain a donkey was within her reach, along with a gift of Christmas joy and forgiveness to cheer up Gill.

*

Trapped with Aunt Evil and *The Sound of Music*, Gill was feeling neither joyful nor forgiving when Petra called suggesting a quick drink later. It was clearly a ruse and typically eleventh hour blasé: 'We've not had a Bags Christmas outing yet! I thought we could try out Broad Compton.'

Gill knew without asking that this had to do with Robbie Marlborough and a donkey.

'I am *not* coming to the pub,' she muttered into her phone. 'I told you my aunt's here. We're going to watch old home movies.'

'I'd love a trip to the pub, dear!' came a plea from the sofa opposite where the sloe gin top-ups were being carefully rationed.

On the other end of the line, Petra sighed dreamily. 'You never mentioned Robbie was so good-looking. Can't you see this is the perfect opportunity to make peace?'

'The answer is no, Petra,' she glared at the television screen where the Von Trapp children were putting on a puppet show.

'Please, Gill, I need your help. The carol singing procession is tomorrow. What happened between you two was donkeys years ago, haha!'

Gill didn't laugh.

'How about a goat?' she offered, watching the hairy puppet herd dancing on TV. 'I have a client whose dressage horse has an unusually tall Saanen companion. Huge ears.'

'Robbie Marlborough has real donkeys. You

should have seen his *eyes* when I mentioned your name, Gill. He looked *so pleased* and so *sad*. Please come out for a drink. Put the past behind you. I'll get the others along.'

'No.'

After ringing off, Gill had difficulty concentrating on *The Sound of Music*. Her phone was already buzzing with a flurry of activity on their WhatsApp riding group. She knew how indiscreet Petra could be. Worse than that, Gill couldn't stop picturing Robbie's sad eyes.

Robbie had always worn his heart on his sleeve, unlike Paul's visored self-containment. He had been so upset when they'd parted ways, he'd insisted on a complete break. Both had honoured that for over three decades, Gill's only transgression a short, polite letter of condolence when his mother had died two years ago. There had been no reply, nor had she expected one. But she had felt his loss acutely.

As Christopher Plummer sang the last line of *Edelweiss* straight to Julie Andrews, she had to stifle a rare sob.

'Please do hush, you're ruining it.' Aunt Evil fished in her bag, thrusting out a crumpled tissue with a cough sweet stuck to it. Then, realising she was sniffing too, she snatched it back to blow her own nose. 'This was darling Ralph's favourite film.'

Evelyn and Ralph's exploding marriage had provided covering fire for Gill's broken engagement all those years ago, its hurled whisky tumblers and screamed accusations of adultery distracting everyone's attention away from her niece's quietly imploding dreams and endless hidden tears.

Aunt Evil was sobbing openly now. 'You have no idea what it feels like to throw away the love of your life, Gill. To lose the man you want to grow old with.'

Going to fetch her aunt a clean tissue, Gill wasn't so sure.

*

Petra received a message from Auriol Bullock with a donkey emoji between two rainbows: *We're relying on you for the star of the show tomorrow, Mrs Gunn*!

All in hand! She replied, trying not to panic.

She felt very let down by the Saddle Bags. Having had no reply to half a dozen urgent WhatsApp requests, she took direct action.

Making her way through Upper Bagot Farm's small evergreen plantation, she burst out between two younger trees crying 'ambush!' to surprise Mo, who was shouldering a six-foot Norwegian spruce.

'Why haven't you replied to my messages?'

'Cos I'm doing this?' Mo suggested kindly, unruffled.

'I need a donkey, Mo.'

'Well, I don't have time to find you one.'

'I know exactly where one is, lots in fact!' Following behind as short, solid Mo carried the tree towards a tumbledown shed at the plantation's edge, she asked how well she knew Robbie Marlborough.

'Never met him.'

'You must have! He's a local farmer.'

'So's Jeremy Clarkson, and I can't say as we're

chums, though my Barry queued behind him at the Esso garage on the Fosse Way once. Said he bought a lot of boiled sweets.'

'So you didn't know he was once engaged to Gill?'

Mo's round, pink face popped up over the fir pines. 'Jeremy Clarkson almost wed Gill?'

'No, this Robbie Marlborough guy. Gill says he can lend me a donkey, but his wife was very officious on the phone, and then I got trapped in a turkey shopping situation up there, so we made a secret assignation, only Gill isn't willing to help even though it's been *years* and Christmas is all about forgiveness and all I need is one –

'What d'you want me to do, Petra?'

'I thought you might know which pub he drinks in for a start?'

'Not a clue,' she looked wary. 'What have you got planned?'

'Pub crawl? The Bags haven't had our Christmas drinks yet.'

'Gill already said no, I bet.'

'I'm worried about her, Mo. Things are bad at home.'

Mo gave her a wise look. They'd all shared enough heartache in the saddle to understand that Gill's larky cynicism hid a painfully uncommunicative marriage. They also knew she hated anyone interfering.

'I just want the donkey.' Petra gave her most pleading look. 'But I'll need a wingman.'

'I'm too busy.'

'I saw your parents on the way in. They said it would do you good to get out.'

'I'll only come if Bridge does.'

'Good job she's already said the same thing.' Petra was certain she would. 'Now I'll have two wings, like a rare breed bird. Just don't say anything to Gill.'

*

The *Sound of Music* had just finished. The sloe gin level was already below the bottle's label, and Aunt Evil had hiccups.

'How about a lie down?' Gill suggested, checking her phone. Paul hadn't replied to her messages, and the clinic switchboard was set to divert to their mobiles at weekends, so there was no point calling. If Aunt Evil had a nap, she could drive across to see if he needed a hand.

'You promised me h-home movies!' Evelyn hiccoughed in protest. Then she took a deep breath, holding it while pinching her nose, turning a worrying shade of purple, eyes bulging.

Concerned her aunt might lose consciousness if she didn't comply, Gill agreed to go and look for them.

The Walcote-Wishes still lived in the same house where Gill had grown up, amongst the oldest in Compton Magna. The original cruck cottage was now a half-timbered endpoint to a family home twice its size, each century adding its stamp. Gill's father Henry Walcote's mixed veterinary surgery had been the cornerstone, which she and Paul had later developed into a specialised practice. When he'd retired, he'd converted his old consulting rooms into a single storey 'grandpa' annexe where he'd hosted lively parties and play readings. This had been used as storage since his death six years earlier. Gill and Paul still harboured plans to make it a teenage space, but with one daughter already at university and two queued, time was running out, and Gill found it hard to muster the steel to clear the space.

There remained a wealth of family memorabilia boxed inside that she was slowly picking her way through. One was her father's cine projector. Neatly labelled with it were more than twenty spools of Super 8. Henry Walcote had been an enthusiastic amateur filmmaker, capturing his young family, horses, amateur drama group and beloved village landscape. Here was over a decade of snippets of Walcote life immortalised from the late sixties to early eighties.

Gill kept meaning to have them transferred to digital format. Paul and the girls weren't interested, but she knew her aunt would like to see them and that it would be a rare treat for her, too. They'd not been looked at since her father's death. Today, with Paul still at the clinic and the girls out with friends, they could indulge in past lives.

They settled in the snug in the oldest crook of the house, Aunt Evil commandeering the sloe gin bottle and a comfortable chair, the family's trio of gundogs claiming the sofas. Gill took down several pictures so she could project against a white wall.

'Shall we start at the beginning?' she suggested, reaching for the one labelled *1970* with fond memories of paddling pools and Dartmoor ponies.

'Lord no, dear!' Aunt Evil exclaimed. '*I'm* not in any of those, and you were a terribly dull child.' Her face brightened as she thought back, her mood instantly supercharged. 'Ralph and I didn't come back from Singapore until seventy-eight. We were here that Christmas! Your father starred in a local panto and threw a party here afterwards. I wore a very fetching Ozzie Clark jumpsuit. Put that one on, Gill, nineteen-seventy-eight. Hurry up!'

Aunt Evil had a zealously demonic look and a significant sloe gin burden, so Gill didn't protest. And a part of her secretly longed to see it too, stomach squirming, knowing what it would reveal. Seventy-eight had been the first year a tall, tawny teenage boy had appeared in the Walcote family footage.

It was the year she and Robbie Marlborough had fallen in love.

PART TWO

'**A**re you sure about this?' Mo fretted as they drove up the single-track lane to Broad Compton.

'Absolutely,' Petra insisted, feeling thrillingly like Sandra Bullock in a heist movie. 'This is Operation Nativity Ass. It's all planned, hey Bridge?'

'Sure, our rare breed man *always* drinks in the Fuzzy Duck in Broad Compton,' confirmed Bridge, an unexpectedly eager recruit to the donkey campaign pub outing, desperate to escape her in-laws. 'Ales knows a fella who knows a fella who knows him.' Her husband was the most sociable Polish builder in the Bardswolds. 'Rumour has it, our man's been propping up the bar looking miserable since the mid-nineties.'

'I knew it!' Petra gasped. 'That's when Gill married Paul!'

'What's that got to do with a donkey?' asked Mo.

'Have you never seen '*It's a Wonderful Life*?' She pointed out, refusing to question whether a cliquey country pub was the best place to approach Robbie Marlborough with two wing women and half a story.

'It don't do to interfere, Petra love.'

'Yeah, and we're no celestial spirit guides,' scoffed Bridge, leaning in between them from the back seat. 'But it's Christmas, ladies, and we need that drink, hee-haw!'

The others hee-hawed back. They had all seen *It's a Wonderful Life*.

*

'Is that chubby thing in sackcloth you, Gill? Your father looks ridiculous in that hat. Is there any more sloe gin? This bottle is almost empty.'

Aunt Evil was loving the home movie show. Having criticised the village's 1978 summer fete, autumn produce show, and the local hunt's opening meet, footage had moved on to the Compton Amateur Drama Society's production of *Mother Goose.* 'What are those birds doing on stage?'

That year, CADS artistic director Henry Walcote – also cast as The Squire – had persuaded poultry farmer Ted Marlborough to supply half a dozen well-behaved Embden geese to accompany King Proper-Gander and Queen Goosegog. This feathered chorus line had been transported to each rehearsal and the subsequent performances by Fred's teenage son, Robbie. He would then hang around shyly chatting up Gill, on holiday from her all-girls sixth form and playing Villager/Gosling/Guest, eager to show off and fall in love.

Their fledgling romance had been captured in perpetuity by the Walcote's Super 8 camera, which had roved around backstage and later filmed the last night jamboree, at which Robbie's tall, rugged father Ted had wowed them all with his hollow legs and jitterbug dance moves.

It was the first time Gill had seen the footage in years, shocked to find herself time-travelling back more than three decades to watch a red-faced seventeen-year-old schoolgirl in pearls dancing to Abba in this sitting room, the Christmas tree in the same corner it was now, greeting cards strung along the ceiling beams.

'Will you look at me!' cried her aunt, admiring her own younger self with a blonde bubble perm and velvet jumpsuit, bopping to *Take a Chance on Me* with a small, elbow-waggling group that included Gill's mother, Aunt Vile and Ted's snake hips. 'I could be one of Pan's People. I *loved* that hair, that look!'

Gill wished she felt the same way about her droopy flick-ups, Laura Ashley smock-dress and pearls. She'd been at least a stone overweight with awful posture. But there was no denying the love in her eyes.

And, my goodness, Robbie had been handsome. Both their cheeks were flaming because they'd just come in from that very long snogging session outside. Their first proper kiss – tongues delightedly tasting each other – after which they had kissed as often as possible for two heavenly years.

'We're like Olivia Newton-John and Travolta!' Aunt Evil admired herself showing off in a spirited jive with Ted Marlborough.

But Gill was still staring at her seventeen-year-old self, a loved-up stranger that first life-changing Christmas with Robbie.

'Freeze frame it there!' Her aunt wailed as her late husband's handsome, watchful face appeared on screen, moustached and side-burned. Ralph was leaning against the mantel, a Staffordshire pottery dog peering over one cashmere shoulder, eyes on the room.

'I can't,' Gill explained as the camera shot panned on round, 'it would melt the film.'

'Ralph was watching me dancing, wasn't he?' Evelyn asked in an excited voice as she appeared onscreen again, striking Saturday Night Fever poses.

'I believe so.' Gill didn't remember Ralph well, just that they'd divorced a few years after this, and he'd died around the same time.

The footage had moved on to the Walcotes on Christmas morning, about to set off to church in the mist, Mum and Dad in ageing houndstooth, Aunt Violet in Gor-Ray and gumboots, Evelyn and Ralph both dashing in fur-trimmed coats and hats amid all the tweed, like two Russian spies. While her aunt waved excitedly at the camera, her husband pulled up his astrakhan collars and looked broodingly into the mid-distance. Gill tried to think who he reminded her of.

'Look at my tiny waist!' Aunt Evil was admiring herself again. 'Of course, I'd been too unhappy to eat most of the year. Our marriage was a mess. One of my greatest regrets, losing that man.'

They watched a lanky figure in a red Jaeger

coat and matching beret cantering after them, flick ups freshly re-tonged, right ear still glowing from pressing the phone receiver to it, sharing a giggly Christmas morning call with Robbie, utterly and hopelessly in love.

'You look like Cardinal Wolsey, Gill darling,' her aunt tittered. 'Did you know he had a mistress?'

'Ralph?'

'No, Wolsey! She was called Joan Larke, and she bore him two children. Men are such scoundrels.'

Gill rechecked her phone, trying not to imagine Paul alone with the practice's prettiest veterinary nurse,

*

Petra was the only one of the three Saddle Bags to have ever been to The Fuzzy Duck, a small lopsided Cotswolds pub sagging prettily between Broad Compton's church and duck pond, its golden limestone walls currently awash with spinning snowflake projections. 'Brace yourselves, it's *very* last year, ladies.'

'Like that comment,' Bridge murmured to Mo as they pulled into the car park.

'I heard that!' she said, offended. 'And I heard the eye rolls.'

Renamed as part of an update to try to attract the wealthy Londonshire set, the smaller of Broad Compton's two pubs had briefly been party central, its once-lively community of locals neglected in favour of cash-splashing second-home owners with a taste for bottled craft ale and a Scottish hunting lodge vibe. But they had already moved on, and tonight, it was half empty, even this close to Christmas. The plaster stag heads, oversized splashy oil paintings and tartan upholstery, garlanded with fake snow and frosted berries, felt like set dressing for a stage play cancelled at the last minute.

The solitary figure perched on an industrial-chic barstool this evening looked very miserable indeed. Once undoubtedly handsome, he was tall, weathered and magnificently wizened, like a kabana sausage in a flat cap.

'He's got to be eighty,' Petra whispered to the others as they peeled off coats by the row of hooks. 'That's not Robbie Marlborough.'

They lined up alongside him to order a round, and Petra leaned across affably. 'Quiet in here tonight!'

'That it is,' he didn't look up.

'Are you waiting for somebody?' she asked hopefully.

A rheumy gaze slid across to her, then on to Bridge and Mo, blinking slowly. 'You three angels come to take me to heaven?'

Bridge started muttering about the old ones being the best.

'Funny you should say that...' Petra elbowed her into silence and sidled closer. 'Is your name Marlborough?'

'Ted Marlborough.' Swallowing audibly, he blinked half a dozen more times, a sparkle lighting up his faded green eyes. '*Is* my name being called?

Am I going to see my Betty again?' It was hard to tell if he was teasing; he was clearly a few rounds ahead of them.

'It's alright, love,' soft-hearted Mo assured him, 'we're just here for a Christmas drink.'

'With an original Marlboro Man,' Bridge joked and got elbowed again.

Chuckling, Ted explained that the family's menfolk had been drinking in this pub for nearly a century: 'Used to have lovely Christmas singsongs in here with my dad and uncles. All dead now, so it's just their ghosts sitting at this bar with me most nights. And now you angels have flown down,' he gazed up at the beamed ceiling, 'fetching me away to meet them and my Betty again, am I right?' A wink was fired sideways at them, suggesting that Ted was more than willing to be corrupted before heading to Heaven.

Petra gave him her most angelic smile. 'Shall we buy you a drink first?'

'How about some tapas?' offered Mo, who was reading the blackboard hungrily.

'Do you have any sons?' demanded Bridge.

Ted looked thrilled.

*

'Is that you on that horse, Gill? Very unflattering things, jodhpurs.'

They had moved onto the Walcote family's 1979 home movie footage, Aunt Evil downing another sloe gin whilst roasting a new round of annual highlights, amongst them a cricket match, hound show, outdoor Shakespeare, a family holiday to Salcombe and the hunter trials at which her niece had won the open class, her handsome boyfriend whooping and fist-pumping her past the finishing flags. Robbie cropped up a lot in 1979, along with his family. Now, he and Gill were do-si-doing at the barn dance, part of a Cornish Hand Reel with Ted and Betty in their sixsome.

'What were you *thinking* of, Gill, getting that pudding bowl haircut?'

'It's a Purdy.' Gill had always rather liked it, matched with a long-collared shirt and fitted waistcoat, considering it her iconic coming-of-age look.

'Oh, there's me again on bonfire night! I'm even thinner! *Fab*ulous fur coat! Vile looks dreadful, poor thing. No fashion sense.'

Aunt Evil also featured surprisingly regularly in these clips, her visits to her brother's family more frequent as her marriage unravelled and her bubble perm dropped, often joined by sister Violet and her home-cut bob. And there was Robbie again, forehead tilted against Gill's, firelight behind them as they unwrapped foil from potatoes baked in its embers, steam rising between them in every sense.

'Who's that thuggish-looking character I keep seeing you with?'

'You remember Robbie?' The centre of her universe had barely registered with Aunt Evelyn, she realised.

'Ah yes, the Pig farmer with disapproving

parents?'

'Heritage poultry. And Ted and Betty were sweet.' She pointed out the tall, robustly handsome, flat-capped figure throwing a pallet on the bonfire while a smaller, cuddlier one waved a sparkler. 'That's them.'

'Good grief, I'd quite forgotten that he – that they – well, I never. Your boyfriend's parents. She's jolly fat, isn't she?'

'You're not supposed to say things like that these days, Evelyn.'

'What's wrong with "jolly"?' Evelyn said naughtily, gasping as the recording jumped forward in time: 'Look at Ralph's face! Cheer up, darling, it's Christmas! I'd hoped we might patch it up that year, but he hardly spoke a word all week. Is that you and your young pig farmer again with a donkey? What *is* he dressed as, Yasser Arafat?'

Gill couldn't bring herself to answer. They were leading the St Mary's Church nativity procession, playing Innkeeper and Wife, a future she'd forsaken.

They'd both known he wanted a way out, so why did she still feel so bad about it?

*

'Daughters are easier than sons,' Ted Marlborough told his 'angels' in the Fuzzy Duck over a freshly pulled pint of a guest ale called Eel Slap. 'I have two what give me no trouble, both wed to farmers.' When Ted had been widowed, he'd let his only son Robert take over the day-to-day running of the family flocks, he explained, 'but that wife of his is always interfering, getting some new-fangled idea.'

'Lindy?' Petra checked.

He nodded and swigged his ale, not questioning how she knew. 'Always liked gobby women, did Robert. My Betty wouldn't say boo to a goose – I should know, we reared tens of thousands of the things – but that woman's a meddler. All them rare breeds she keeps introducing, goats one minute, mouflon the next, applying for some grant or other. We're poultry farmers, always have been! Now she wants to make biltong and cheese and offer yurts and all sorts of nonsense. She's away with the fairies, that one. Women!' Chuckling and tutting, Ted raised his pint to his lips again.

'Woah, wee fella, that's feck–'

'She also breeds donkeys, I gather?' Petra cut across Bridge, trying to steer him on track, hoping the sisterhood would forgive her.

'Little donkeys,' Mo repeated for emphasis, a trusty corporal.

'No, they was my Betty's,' his eyes went misty. 'She loved them little asses, did Betty.' His daughter-in-law had a more undomesticated approach, he explained. 'Lets them run wild, Lindy does.'

'Does nobody handle them?' Petra asked anxiously.

'Not lately.' He sighed. 'I'm not as steady as I was, see, and Robbie's too busy with the birds. Breaks my heart nobody loves them like my Betty. Savages, half of them. Not wanted, poor little blighters.'

'Have you thought about contacting Silver

Hooves Sanctuary?' Petra decided the back end of a panto costume was quite tempting after all.

'They *are* wanted, Ted!' Kind-hearted Mo was appalled. 'That's why we're here.'

'Just the one donkey, Mo, ' Petra reminded her tightly, 'a very placid one on loan for a night.'

'And there was me thinking you ladies are here to take me up to heaven to be with my Betty again,' he sighed, crinkling his eyes at them.

'Heaven can wait, Ted!' Bridge was in a rabble-rousing mood. 'Which with your sexist attitude, will probably be an etern–'

'We need a donkey!' Mo cried.

'Fair enough,' Ted gave them another twinkly look, picking up his pint and draining it. 'In that case, I'll have another of these while we strike a deal, my angels. With a whisky chaser this time, perhaps?'

'You know what scotch does to you, Dad!' A husky voice protested behind them.

The three Bags turned as one, drawing a synchronised breath at the sheer size and scale of Robbie Marlborough.

'Well, hello again, Bob.' Petra took in the thick, peppery pelt and contrasting auburn stubble. Without his white hat and hairnet, he was even more impressive.

He eyed her with tired amusement as he shrugged off his long stock coat. 'You came to the poultry shed earlier.'

'That's right,' she beamed, noting the

Herculean shoulders in a novelty Christmas jumper.

'Robert, these are my angels,' Ted told his son.

'Did this one tell you she's a friend of Gill Walcote's,' Robbie nodded at Petra.

Ted almost fell off his stool. 'In that case, you're not getting your hands on my wife's herd – or my soul come to that!'

*

Spooling the reel labelled *1980* on the cine projector, Gill heard the sound of the front door, the thwack of oak against frame loud enough to suggest Paul was still in a black mood.

The dogs scrabbled off the sofas to greet him as he put his head around the snug door to demand to know where the girls were. Gill could only offer 'out' although she knew they were safe enough, messages pinging in from friends' houses at regular intervals.

'We're watching reels!' Aunt Evil told him, her volume still stuck at max. 'Back when Gill was going to marry the handsome pig farmer!'

'Heritage poultry,' Gill muttered, seeing Paul's frown deepen. He knew about Robbie, of course, although they hadn't spoken of it for decades, both their past romances archived. She worried their mutual one was, too.

'Shall we stop there?' she suggested to her aunt, relieved. Nineteen-eighty was not a year she cared to relive, besides which the heat from the wood burner - roaring at full tilt to keep Evelyn warm - had triggered a dreaded hot flush that refused to budge.

'Absolutely not! Come and join us!' Aunt Evil

was full of sloe gin largesse, waving a hand from Paul to the sofa the dogs were already reclaiming. 'Gill's treating me to a jaunt along memory lane. I was a stunner at her age. Could you fix us a couple of sundowners, Ralph darling – G and Ts maybe?'

'I have work to do. I'm still on call. Someone must stay sober. And it's Paul.' He shot them both a dirty look and stalked out.

'Oops!' Evelyn widened her eyes in mock horror, chortling at her gaffe. 'Ralph was an uptight sort, too. *Very* serious about work. Terribly alike in that respect, don't you think?'

Fanning her face with a tape box, Gill realised with a jolt who Aunt Evil's unhappy, tight-lipped late husband reminded her of. Her own unhappy, tight-lipped one.

'Bring on the eighties!' Evelyn ordered, waving a hand at the projector.

*

'Why d'you want to know about my Betty's donkeys?' Ted had cast aside flirty patter and was eyeing the Bags with rheumy suspicion, only slightly placated by another pint of Eel Slap. Standing behind him, his man-mountain of a Christmas-jumpered son was nursing a large glass of Malbec, which struck Petra as endearingly incongruous because it was Gill's favourite tipple, plus her lovely, grumbly vet friend was still the first to don her Fleece Navidad hoody and reindeer antler helmet silk to ride out in. How perfect they might have been together had things panned out differently.

Petra put her plea for the loan of a donkey on behalf of the local vicar and the village headmistress, casting herself as their saintly emissary and emphasising that vet Gill had merely passed on the tip, wanting no part of it.

'She told me they're beautifully bred,' she enthused, looking to her fellow Bags for wing-women support.

'Yes, really sweet,' Mo backed her up.

'But she said that your turkeys taste way better,' Bridge polished off her Guinness, still smarting over Ted's sexist comments.

Petra's smile fixed.

'Gill know what they're called, does she?' Ted demanded.

Petra wasn't sure how to answer this. 'Should she?'

He harrumphed, knocking back more Eel Slap.

Petra refused to give up, sensing the charm offensive needed a turbo boost.

'You had so many customers today!' she deflected, beaming from father to son. 'The Harrods of the Comptons. What a team!'

'Yeah, we got all the local bird orders collected.' Robbie gave her a look that hinted why Gill had once been smitten, blue-green eyes all-knowing. He raised his glass to Ted, stifling a yawn. 'Thanks for all your help earlier, Dad.'

Ted raised his in return, somewhat mollified, telling the others: 'Me and my Betty used to pluck them all ourselves back in the day, but I just get in the way now with this arthritis.'

'We couldn't do it without Dad sorting them,' Robbie put a big hand on his shoulder.

'I bet you do!' Petra guessed Ted had been the helper he'd been calling to out of sight in the barn earlier. 'Your farm is *lovely*,' she added, eager to win them both round.

'Been tenanted by Marlboroughs for ten generations.' Ted said proudly, some of the old gusto returning.

'Gill really send you up to our place today?' Robbie asked, his eyes doing their intense green thing, which Petra secretly found rather thrilling, still finessing her battle-worn Napoleonic war general.

'Entirely my idea.' She knew she must tread carefully.

But Bridge was already on her second pint of Guinness: 'I can't believe you're just a village away and she's never mentioned you. That's batshit, that is! An ex-fiancé! She's always been a dark horse, Gill.'

'Trouble's what she is.' Ted looked thunderous once more. 'Always was hoity toity, Henry Walcote's girl. Had a lucky escape there.' He told his son, who looked down at his wine, saying nothing.

'Gill's lovely,' Mo told them brightly, munching her way through the tapas order that had just arrived. 'A bit bossy, granted, and don't get her onto worming rotations because she never shuts up, but she's got as big a heart as they come.'

'Must've grown one,' Ted muttered.

'What did the woman do to you?' Bridge demanded.

Ted placed his pint on the bar and wiped his lip. 'She broke all our hearts. That's what she did.'

*

'Awful dress...that vicar has a look of Peter Sutcliffe...what dreadful legs... perms like that are never flattering over forty...should have wired those jaws...'

Aunt Evil was on a roll as the Super 8 projector whirred and purred through nineteen-eighty's fetes and garden parties, the scarecrow competition, a family holiday on the Norfolk Broads and Broadbourne Horse Show. Throughout the year, Gill realised her look had increasingly morphed to Lady Diana Spencer, who had careered into everyone's heart that summer with her shy smile, Mini Metro and see-through skirt. In Compton Magna, the teenage pearls had started wrapping themselves around Gill's pie-crust collars, the Size 8 ballet pumps making regular appearances, the cheeks always stained pink with love. Almost constantly at her side, Robbie grew ever more handsome and imposing in double denim and checked cotton, the boy filling out to man, now six feet four, her protector and best friend.

By September, Gill was sporting his grandmother's cushion-cut emerald on her ring finger. He'd proposed on one knee, high up on the Compton ridgeway by the old windmill, from where they could see dust clouds above the combines cutting wheat between their two villages. By then, she'd got her A-level results, and they knew she would be off to veterinary college. He would be her anchor and safe harbour. But first, a gap year. *Their* year.

Their respective families were cautiously supportive, pointing out they were very young to make such a commitment but aware of how much they worshipped one another. The Walcotes saw Robbie as a true countryman to keep their daughter grounded. And the Marlboroughs adored Gill, with gentle, self-effacing Betty insisting a strong female was just what the family needed, admiring Gill's ability to put her thoughts into words and call the shots: 'Our Robbie could use a wife that's clever and articulated. Don't want him turning out a bad'un like his dad.' They'd all laughed uproariously at this, Ted loudest of all.

And Gill and Robbie were nothing like Ted and Betty, who had been parents by twenty. They were sensible; there was no plan to marry quickly. They'd both been virgins and wanted to keep it that way for now. At least Gill did, and Robbie had reluctantly accepted this after a few fumbling, over-eager seduction attempts in his car that had made them both feel a bit awkward afterwards. Had she subconsciously guessed he was soon having second thoughts, Gill wondered now, watching herself and Robbie side-by-side raising a toast at her mother's fiftieth birthday. Had the worm of doubt already been eating its way inside her here? If so, after Betty had spoken with her, it became a hydra.

'Oh, look at me in my Roland Klein!' Aunt Evil cried as the tree, paperchains, and cracker hats flickered on the projection once again. 'Our last visit here together. I was a size eight! That was some sort of charity concert at the village hall, wasn't it? Your father sang *White Christmas*, and then we all went outside and realised it was! Snow everywhere. See, there we are at the carol singing the next day. There's dear, miserable Ralph. Such a filthy look he's giving us all. Isn't my camelhair coat gorgeous?'

But Gill could only see Robbie, his kissable mouth smiling and singing as everyone belted out *Oh Come All Ye Faithful* on the village green, unaware his Christmas cheer would be shattered later that evening.

She jumped as she felt a warm, softly wrinkled hand slip into hers. 'Ralph had packed his bags and gone by New Year.' The last of the sloe gin was drained from Evelyn's crystal glass. 'If I could travel back and stop him leaving that Christmas, I would. You know he died of a heart attack the day our divorce came through?'

To Gill's surprise, her aunt burst into loud sobs.

She reached for the tissues mini pack, extracting one for herself before passing them across. They blew their noses in unison.

It only now occurred to Gill that the memory of Christmas nineteen-eighty might be just as painful to Evelyn.

'Can we watch it again, Gill darling?'

'Why would you want to if it makes you unhappy?'

'Because it makes me see that I had the choice to change everything once. When you're as old as me, and you've come to feel as powerless, that's jolly cathartic.' The warm hand retook hers and squeezed it tightly.

Gill looked at her aunt in alarm, hoping she would never come to this.

'And I really did look *very* lovely, didn't I?' Evelyn added with a mischievous giggle, which turned into a wistful sigh.

*

'Called it off without a by your leave, she did,' Ted told them. 'Destroyed your faith, din it, Robert?'

'I got over it,' he said gruffly, hugely uncomfortable.

'Gill was like family.' Ted shook his head. 'My Betty worshipped her. We was shocked through, as you can imagine, Petra.'

'Absolutely.'

In truth, Petra didn't find it hard to picture no-nonsense eighteen-year-old Gill telling her fiancé she must put her studies first, having recently witnessed her pragmatically lecturing her loved-up oldest daughter to do just that.

What Petra did find odd was that she'd done so on Christmas Eve. Gill might be bah-humbug about Christmas this year, but she was secretly more sentimental about its festivities than anyone Petra knew, and had enough Christian faith to wish no ill will or unhappiness on the one day universally acknowledged to bring much-needed joy.

The timing didn't make much sense at all.

*

Aunt Evil made Gill play the Christmas 1980 home movie twice through again, each time getting more tearful, starting to ramble as her sloe gin overload peaked. 'You can *see* how desperate Ralph was for a sign of hope, can't you? Everybody thought he was arrogant, but he was a shy man, socially awkward. He was simply overshadowed by my charisma and popularity. You can witness that here, can't you? Look at his face, watching me like a hawk. He hated me flirting with other men – he was suspicious of everybody – and I only did it to make him jealous, although that was very foolish, I see it now. He was just *so* aloof. And I was *vibrant*.'

Gill said diplomatically that her aunt was a big personality to live up to.

'Of course, things might have been different if we'd had children, but then again, if we'd had those, I might not be left alone in that ghastly geriatric prison I'm in now. I'd have close family and support, who knows maybe grandchildren, perhaps even an annexe like your father had here. Is that in use at all?'

Gill told her that it was, yes, very much in use and suggested her aunt might like that little lie down while she cooked supper?

Aunt Evil wanted a gin and tonic, thank you,

following her into the kitchen and weaving around its flagstones, looking at family photographs on the walls. 'Your father was always blessed with good fortune. You have inherited that with your family here, your vocation. And you married the right man, Gill – that little Kiwi is a keeper. Stoic, hard worker, still trim. He'll look after you in old age. Never marry for love, that's my motto – it's so unreliable.' She peered at Gill and Paul's wedding photograph on the Welsh dresser, taken on the church steps with him one step up from her, closer to God, to disguise that he was several inches shorter. '*Awful* hair.'

'Mine or his?'

'Both. Perfectly matched, you see! You should see mine and Ralph's wedding album – we look like Sonny and Cher. Beautiful but doomed! You found your level –' the word hung there as an insult while her thoughts caught up, 'your level-headed chum.'

Gill said nothing, too acutely aware of Paul brooding in his study right now, his Berlin wall of a back waiting in bed later, his ever-present, joy-sapping irritation. Aware also that she kept another man's ring in her jewellery box. And that Aunt Evil was now standing very close to her, peering up at her face.

'*Is* everything all right between you two, Gill?'

She was immensely grateful that the girls chose that moment to arrive noisily home, both thrilled to find the projector out in the snug.

'Oh, *please* show us those shots of life here in the olden days!' One begged, while the other rushed round for snacks and checked the state of the great slab of lasagne Gill had only just slammed in the Aga. 'This won't be ready for *ages*. Let's watch some!' They skipped off to the snug, dogs scurrying and Evelyn reeling in their wake.

'I thought you found them boring?' Gill called after them.

'Not now the fashion's come back round. Come *on*, Mum!'

'One more time!' Aunt Evil was already back in position, now with a complete gin mixing kit on the occasional table beside her.

Forced to watch her last days together with Robbie all over again, Gill found it an entirely different experience with a body-positive crowd alongside:

'Ohmygod, Mum, you are *gorgeous*!'

'Look at your rock chick hair! And how *trendy* were you! That's some drip! What are those things on your legs?'

'Culottes,' she said, perching on a chair arm because all the seats were now taken, mostly by daughter and dogs. 'And according to you they're coming around again.' She could hear the Carly Simon song in her head.

'You totally rock them, but trust me, Mum, those things will *never* come around again.'

Like second chances at love, thought Gill as Robbie's face flickered into view again.

One daughter let out a shriek: 'Who's *he*? *Fit!* OMG, he's like something out of *Footloose*. I wish we'd lived back then!'

She braced herself for the Christmas footage; the Walcote and Marlborough families united for both the village hall Christmas concert and the carol singing on the Green the following afternoon. This time, Gill saw the transformation between her happy, smiling face one day and her wretched mask the next, the conversation she'd had with Betty Marlborough between the two changing everything.

'Aunt Evil, I totally heart your camel hair coat.'

'Isn't it just divine? Jackie Onassis had the exact same one. Darling Ralph bought it for me.'

And there was Ralph, shooting that legendary filthy look. But it wasn't aimed at his vibrant blonde wife or her extended family, Gill realised. He was glaring at the Marlboroughs.

Her daughters were enthralled by the lo-fi last century authenticity of it all. '*And* it was a white Christmas that year! It looks so pretty and so thick! There's someone in *snow*shoes.'

It's why she hadn't been able to go after Robbie when he'd stormed off, Gill remembered. She'd wanted to explain everything better, to give him back the ring and beg his forgiveness. But her Mini Metro had got stuck just a few yards from the end of her own drive.

*

'Who wants to give an old man a Christmas kiss under the mistletoe before he's taken to Heaven?' Armed with another pint of Eel Slap, Ted Marlborough was back in festive spirits.

With no takers, he tucked happily into a plate of patatas bravas instead, hailing familiar faces across The Fuzzy Duck's bar room.

The pub was filling up with villagers willing to temporarily forgive the pound-shop private members' club décor for the sake of neighbours, visiting families and the legendary spiced cider served at this time of year. Christmas music was being piped over the speakers, and some were having a singalong, a spontaneous round of *The Twelve Days of Christmas* breaking out.

But Petra's Operation Nativity Ass donkey campaign was meeting rugged opposition.

Robbie was on his second Malbec, red-cheeked and bright-eyed, shouting at her over the pipers piping. 'They don't like being separated, the donkeys. Herd mentality, you know?'

'What if we use herbal calmer?'

'*Drug* them?' He gave her a bemused look, eyebrow raised.

'It's totally natural. Gill recommended it for my mare. Works wonders.'

"*Fiiiiive gooold riiiings*" drowned out his reply, but Petra thought she heard: 'might try some on the wife.'

Beside her, Mo was too busy munching calamari to be paying attention, and Bridge was on her feet with the locals hailing two turtle doves at top voice.

Petra clearly heard what Robbie said next: 'If Gill wants one of Mum's donkeys so much, tell her to ask me herself.'

'Actually, it's me who wants to borrow one,' she reminded him, leaning closer to be heard over another noisy countdown from maids a-milking, 'for tomorrow's carol singing procession.'

He leaned in, too, until their noses were almost touching, 'They still do that down in Compton Magna?'

'They're reviving it this year.'

He smiled slowly, sea-green eyes at their most intense. 'Tell you what, bring Gill up to the farm in the morning and let her pick one out. If she can tell me its name, it's yours.'

*

On a full-scale nostalgia bender, Aunt Evil rambled talkatively throughout supper, now modestly sipping sparkling English wine, her many anecdotes veering off at slurred tangents, which an emotionally drained Gill found exhausting. Paul ignored her completely. But their girls were chatty and kind, happy to deflect and flatter and ask questions and listen.

'In Monaco with Onassis, we were treated to the most extraordinary *son et lumiere*...travelling up the Nile by sailboat with Taylor and Burton was rather a treat...then the Aga Khan invited Ralph to throw in the first polo ball with Charles bouncing about on the freshest pony you've ever seen...'

Gill suspected a few were made up. Others were embellished, but many were peppered with authentic details, and the girls loved them.

For the first time, she realised there were whole sections of her aunt's life she'd never known about, her years accompanying glamorous attaché Ralph around exotic locations, her love of travel, her lost friendships and communities, and her life's golden era now reduced to a vintage Wicker's World anachronism. They had even visited New Zealand for several months, she told Paul eagerly. 'Quite my favourite colony, Peter!'

Still he said nothing, but his gaze flickered briefly across Gill's while their girls tactfully updated Evelyn on their twenty-first-century worldview, bigging up the many ways their father's country of origin was ahead of Britain in its progress and thinking, then steering her onto the safer subjects of film and fashion.

'Oh yes – at one Bond Premiere, I wore such a tightly corseted Belville Sassoon that when Warren Beattie slipped his number into my cleavage with a witty line, it popped straight back out again the moment I laughed! Ralph was livid when he saw it flutter past. He was always *so* jealous, have I said?'

'Just a few times,' muttered Gill, looking at Paul.

But the girls were lapping it up, demanding to know about other parties and premieres.

Gill continued watching her husband as he ate, remembering Evelyn's words. *You married the right man.*

They had made this family. Their kind daughters.

He glanced up at her.

We are so lucky to have them, she told him silently. We did a good job raising them. They will soon fly away to enjoy their adult lives. We must learn to talk to each other again as friends, not just colleagues, to like one another again, love even.

She tried to convey every word in one long eye meet, appalled to find her rare tears rising again.

Frowning, he turned away to answer his ringing phone, clearly grateful for the distraction. A suspected colic would take him out on an emergency visit, he told them with relief, thanking Gill politely for supper before almost sprinting for the door.

After eating, the girls took Aunt Evil to the snug to watch *The Holiday,* promising they'd wash up later.

Glancing at the clock, astonished to find it wasn't yet nine, Gill tracked down her phone and called Paul to see if he needed help. It went to voicemail. He'd message her if he did, she reminded herself.

Just like Petra had: *Please come to Broad Comption with me tomorrow? My ass depends on it!* She'd added a lot of namaste emojis.

Gill swiped it aside. There was no way she was opening that advent calendar door, even if, as she suspected, nothing lay beyond it but ancient history and donkeys. She owed it to Paul to leave the past alone, their marital bad patch tough enough without scratching through her past any more than she just had.

She put the supper things in soak and

stored away the leftovers before heading outside, heart-lifting as always at the euphoric whickering welcome in her little yard. She topped up hay and water, then pressed her forehead to the soft, solid warmth of horse neck, leaning in to breathe his goodness.

She wasn't sure how long she'd been there when a voice over the door made them both jump. 'You always were pony mad.'

It was Aunt Evil, wearing two coats and a woolly hat almost down over her eyes. 'Came to say goodnight.' She sounded woozy.

It was frosty outside, and Gill worried she might fall. 'I'll be in in a minute.'

'Wanted to see the stars,' she stepped back, lurching slightly, and looked up, hugging herself for warmth. 'Aways like to imagine Ralph up there. Lovely to see him again earlier. I do miss having a husband, but I never found another to match him. Or they belonged to someone else.' She sighed, pitching forward to look over the door again and pat the gelding haphazardly on the forehead. 'Do you have just the one?'

'Husband?'

'Horse.'

'Yes.'

'Must be lonely, poor creature. They're sociable animals, aren't they, like us? It's horrid being alone.'

Gill felt the weight of the pause, the guilty obligation to offer her aunt a longer stay, more visits, more space in their busy lives.

But Evelyn was talking again, her agenda quite different: 'Far lonelier being with somebody who acts like you're not there, who doesn't *see* you, don't you think? Off to bed now. Tootle pip.' She reeled around, weaving away across the yard, calling, 'I'll find my own way back!' and walking into the feed room.

Gill hurried out to see her into the house and up to bed, ensuring she had plenty of water and Alka Seltzer lined up.

It was almost midnight when Paul got back, and everyone was in bed, only the dogs skittering around on the flagstones downstairs in delirious welcome.

Gill was still awake, rolling to face him when he got in, catching him before he turned his back to her. 'Can we make friends?'

He punched a dent in the pillow to sink his head in. 'I'm too tired.'

'I said make friends, Paul, not love.'

He didn't answer, rolling away to raise the familiar cliff face of his back to her.

Gill got up to go to the loo to pee, *not* to cry, although it was practical to quietly dab her eyes and blow her nose in the unlit privacy of the en suite. She refused to submit to self-pity. He was bound to be tired. He'd been with a colicking horse for three hours.

She jumped when something lit up on the vanity unit with a brief hornet buzz. Paul had left his phone beside the basin, its sleep screen showing an incoming message alert. Gill recognised the name of their prettiest veterinary nurse, a lean-thighed eventing fanatic. There was no way she could break through her security-mad husband's face-recognition fingerprinted biometrics, but she could see the first line of her message. *Of course I won't tell Gill our secret...*

At one a.m., she was still lying awake, past, present and future running through her head like the cine player's flickering projections, her insomnia reaching new panic peaks.

She picked up her own phone and reread the message Petra had sent earlier: *Please come to Broad Compton with me tomorrow? My ass depends on it!*

She typed *okay* and pressed the green arrow.

PART THREE

By morning, Gill had developed seriously cold feet, and not just because the boiler packed up at dawn, coinciding with a blistering chill blowing in from the north. Paul's 'you deal with it' departure to the clinic left her hobbled.

'I have to stay here and wait for an engineer,' she rang Petra.

'We'll be there and back before you know it. Please, Gill. The carol singing is tonight! And there's something else…'

Leaving the family crowding around the Aga for warmth, Gill put an extra rug on her gelding, who lent affectionately against her, hooking his big jaw over her shoulder and letting out a deep sigh, resigned to another solitary day.

'We'll have an adventure soon,' she promised, wishing she could remain here to enjoy a long ride together, blasting off cobwebs along the three-mile point on an imaginary quest.

Instead, Gill had just been tasked with a real one. The challenge Petra had just relayed on the phone seemed ridiculous. 'If you correctly guess the name of any donkey, you will save my bacon!'

Gill had absolutely no idea what Betty Marlborough had called any of her beloved herd in the eighties, let alone before she died two years ago. Whilst starry-eyed Petra saw it as a Christmas fairytale adventure, she feared a practical joke at her expense.

By the time they set off, she was in a muck sweat despite the cold. Was this a forfeit for her decades of silence?

'This is ridiculous.' She muttered at Petra as they drove up the narrow lane linking Compton Bagot and Broad Compton, the window beside her steaming up. 'The emergency plumber could turn up any time. I have a million things to do, and Paul is manning the clinic single-handed.' No need to mention that neither of them was scheduled to be there that morning unless called in for an emergency.

'It's Sunday,' Petra waved a dismissive hand, 'it's not like there are any appointments. The carol singing is *tonight*. Have you thought of any names yet?'

'Rumpelstiltskin?' she muttered.

'El Rucio?' A suggestion came from the back seat. Aunt Evil had invited herself along, complaining the house was too cold. 'He was Sancho Panzo's donkey. *Such* a treat to be out, hey girls? Any donkey name ideas?'

Also escaping the cold, Gill's daughters were sitting on either side of their great aunt, fully invested in Operation Nativity Ass and only partially aware of the delicacy of their mother's situation.

'Honkey?'

'Tonkey!'

An excited bark reminded Gill that Petra's spaniel Wilf was also coming along for the ride.

The pony trailer rattled behind the car as they crossed a cattle grate onto Compton Common.

At first, Gill had thought bringing her family along would act as a protective human shield to make this feel normal, but it just made it worse, like arriving in a circus cavalcade.

She glanced over her shoulder at Aunt Evil, marvelling at her powers of recovery. She was gripping her hydro flask, resplendent in a turquoise velour tracksuit, pink down jacket and dark glasses, announcing grandly that it was going to snow.

'Do you think so?' one of Gill's daughters asked excitedly, staring at the cold grey clouds and then down at her phone. 'My app doesn't say so. What makes you instinctively know?'

'Ladbrokes are giving it odds on.' Aunt Evil gave Gill a wise look over her shades, her gaze remarkably bright.

Closing her eyes, Gill prayed for a quick blizzard, forcing them to turn back. She'd drunk nothing the previous evening, and yet her skull was being crushed. By burying her worries about Paul so deeply, she'd displaced her past life, which now yawned like an open wound.

We will never speak again, Robbie Marlborough

had said as the snow thickened almost forty years ago, white flakes on his collar, in his hair, his lashes, his voice frozen tight with hurt. *Not one word, ever.*

Gill hadn't believed it possible, yet they had made it through every intervening decade without a word exchanged.

It had been easy at first, when the pain was most acute, her gap year VSO taking her to Africa for six months, followed by six years of veterinary study, only home for flying visits. By the time she'd joined her father's practice, Gill's brief betrothal belonged to another era and community, the widespread Comptons villages rapidly divided and diluted by new blood and new builds. The Walcotes and Marlboroughs had no mutual friends; Ted and Betty had stopped using Henry Walcote's veterinary services as soon as the engagement ended; the farming family worshipped at a different church; they weren't involved with horses and the hunt like the Walcotes. When the farm's rare breeds expanded from poultry to livestock, they attracted local press attention, winning awards and hosting open days, but Gill had never gone.

Despite living just a few miles apart, she and Robbie had encountered each other half a dozen times at most, neither acknowledging the other.

She'd only found out he'd married when she'd chanced across a notice in the local paper, placed there by Betty and Ted. *Marlborough, Robert and Lindy. Happy Tenth Wedding Anniversary, love and best wishes, Mum and Dad.*

Tenth! That day, Gill had felt a bomb go off in her chest. She was still single, but he'd married within a year of her breaking off the engagement. It was, she would later realise, the moment she let go of the ridiculous hope that Robbie might know she hadn't meant a word she'd said.

At the time, the Walcotes had a bright young New Zealand vet on a year's work placement. Paul Wish made no secret of his quiet crush on Gill. Aside from a few undergraduate fumbles and a long, sexless round of dinner dates and hunt balls with a dull Scottish horse dentist, she had barely kissed a man since Robbie. It was the way Paul called horses 'neds' – pronounced 'nids' – that first melted her heart. Determined to finally move on, she'd embraced coupledom, delighted to find a flinty toughness beneath Paul's kitten fur, matched with fearlessness in the saddle. They'd married two years later, theirs a formidable professional partnership, if privately more diffident.

It had taken the Walcote-Wishes over a decade of empire-building before starting a family, by which time Gill had been in her late thirties, biological clock on repeat. Their three daughters arrived in rapid succession; unconditional mother love had proved the perfect antidote for marital shyness. For her final pregnancy, awaiting her twenty-week hospital scan, Gill had looked up in shock from a well-thumbed *Take A Break* to hear the nurse call 'Marlborough!'. She was even more surprised to find the expectant mother was barely eighteen, with familiar green eyes and dimpled chin. With her was a fierce, handsome woman in place of a co-parent.

They had to be Robbie's daughter and wife, Gill had guessed. It was as close as she'd ever been to his family.

Until today, when, to her consternation, they were greeted by the same tall, ruddy-faced woman she remembered guarding her pregnant daughter. Her mane of curls was now grey, her tall, rangy body thickened out. Striking in dungarees and a gypsy shirt, like a sexy ageing member of Bananarama, she had a voice that could carry three fields.

'I'm Lindy, great to meetcha!' She offered a gap-toothed smile and wrist-breaking handshake first to Petra, then Gill, who felt her finger bones crunch, before she and the others were beckoned towards the thatched farmhouse she remembered so well.

Lindy walked with a shoulder-swaying swagger, 'Bob said to expect you. He's still out on the farm. Come in and have a cuppa while you wait! You're here for the donkey herd, yeah?'

'Oh, I *do* love donkeys!' Aunty Evil let out a cry of joy. 'Ralph used to say I'd talked the hind legs off one. Tell me, what is that accent? Are you from New Zealand like Gill's boring husband?'

*

Petra had immediately taken to Gill's parrot-bright aunt, Evelyn. She was splendidly show-stealing, the grande dame manner in which she took each great-niece by the arm as they entered the cosy farmhouse. 'I must sit down! What *is* this place, Hobbiton?'

But she was nothing to Lindy Marlborough's big decibel welcome, leading them through a maze of wonky, oak-panelled corridors. 'Been dying to see the back of those greedy little asses, I don't mind telling you. No profit in them!'

She was a woman transformed away from the stress of her annual Christmas poultry collection, with a generous, boho energy, her language as colourful as her home, beckoning Aunt Evil into her kitchen ahead of the others. 'Park your arse there while I brew up, love! You need something sugary as sin, yah!'

If Lindy recognised Petra as the wreath-grabbing interloper, she wasn't saying. The fact she seemed to think they were here to take away *all* the donkeys and not just borrow one was a worry, but Petra was confident they could smooth that out.

Inside, the farmhouse was an upcycled make-do-and-mend palace of festive cheer. Its low-beamed rooms were crammed with clashing prints, pottery, scrubbed oak and contented cats, the Christmas decorations bursting with greenery, berries and teasels. The kitchen smelled of home baking, roasting gammon, hot toddies and drying herbs. And it was toasty warm, seasoned logs crackling in a wood burner at one end, an ancient, scuffed cream Rayburn pumping out heat at the other.

'This is very homely,' Evelyn had turned as bright pink as her coat.

'Still can't take the English cold after forty years!' boomed Lindy, who told them she was South African, from Northern Cape farming stock, and although her accent had been all but subsumed by the Bardswolds burr, 'my folks back home all now reckon I sound like Olivia Coleman!'

She was also unexpectedly upfront, addressing Gill over her shoulder as she filled the kettle: 'Always wanted to meet you. No idea you lived so close. Me and Bob met soon after you two split. He talked more about you than this farm that first year, but I figured he'd grow out of it soon enough, and he did. You're smaller than I imagined. Way Bob describes you, I thought you'd be butch as a wrestler.'

Petra rarely saw Gill lost for words. The two Walcote-Wish daughters were also open-mouthed with surprise.

Aunt Evil let out a tremulous gasp, rigid in her ladder-back carver chair by the table: 'Gill, are we in the *pig farmers'* house?'

'Heritage poultry,' muttered Gill.

'And is he still alive?' Evelyn gripped the table edge.

'Course he is!' Lindy scoffed, plonking the kettle on the range's hot plate. 'The man's a bull, love. He didn't die of a broken heart, love.'

'My husband did!' Aunt Evil's pink cheeks were fast draining of colour.

Gill gave a tight, embarrassed smile. 'Not now, Evelyn.'

'All my stupid fault.'

'What haven't you told us, Great Aunt Evil?' one of Gill's daughters laughed nervously.

'I as good as signed darling Ralph's death sentence that wretched Christmas!' wailed Aunt Evil, unscrewing her hydro flask and taking a long draught. '*Now* you bring me here, Gill.'

'Kill the Christmas vibe, why doncha, love?' Lindy let out her cheery bellow of laughter. 'At least try one of my Stollen bites.'

'Evelyn's just feeling a bit overwhelmed,' Gill gave her aunt a comforting pat, much as she would a pony she was about to jab, shooting Petra another this-was-your-stupid-idea look.

But Petra was enchanted, half wondering if Evelyn was about to confess to a crime of passion as the old lady repeated, 'All my silly fault!'

'Tell you what, come through and sit by the fire - meet my grandson, Travis,' Lindy led them through a doorway to a sitting room crammed with yet more brightly hand-painted and upholstered furniture, where a good-looking boy who was curled up on a patchwork sofa, pulling headphones from his ears to smile languidly up at them.

'Yo.' Travis had the most heart-melting eyes.

'Travis'll keep you company while Gill and I make that pot of tea.'

It didn't escape Petra's notice, the casual way Lindy included Gill in this action. However, she was temporarily distracted by this rare specimen of beautiful youth, already mentally casting him as a page to a lonely, imprisoned young queen in her next novel. Beside her, Gill's daughters were both sizing him up like a man-sized Belgian chocolate reindeer.

'Excuse me!' Evelyn was still lingering in the kitchen. 'I wonder if I have something stronger?'

Petra turned to see Gill stalking after Lindy into the kitchen, shushing her aunt, 'It's *far* too early for a drink, Aunt Evil!'

Travis clicked his tongue in amusement. 'Is she really called Aunty Evil?'

'You should meet Uncle Sadist and Cousin Mad Bastard,' one of Gill's daughters slid in beside him.

The other claimed the sofa arm on Travis's unmarked side, smiling brightly. 'Do your parents live here too?'

'Mum died; I don't know my dad.'

'Yikes, I'm so sorry. Insensitive of me to ask.'

'Not at all,' the melting eyes smiled into hers. 'It's my best chat up line, along with "my name's Travis, but you can call me tonight".'

As a Walcote-Wish daughter melted either side of him, Petra suspected she might have underestimated the power of Marlborough men. She hoped bringing Gill here wasn't a terrible mistake.

*

'Aunt Evelyn's a bit off colour,' Gill apologised to Lindy as her aunt knocked back two paracetamol with her hydro-flask. 'I'm so sorry we've all imposed on you like this.'

She wished she hadn't agreed to come to the farm, now a sugar-glazed confection of homespun

Christmas cheer on a shoestring, complete with sexy, crafting-mad Mrs Cratchit.

Lindy was no meek, kindly Betty Marlborough.

'Not at all!' Lindy flashed her weapon-grade smile. 'As I said, I was hoping to meet you.' She pulled the whistling kettle from the hot plate. 'Say my piece.' She swept past with the kettle, forcing Gill to step back from its scorch-steam of heat.

'Yes, it's good to have this opportunity to make peace.' Gill rephrased, trusting that's what she meant. Then she swallowed uncomfortably when Lindy glanced over her shoulder with a Jack Nicholson smile that suggested it wasn't.

Composure recovered, Aunt Evil straightened her velour tracksuit zip and patted her hair. May I use your lavatory, Linda?'

'I'll show you the way.' While they were gone, Gill looked for family photos, hoping to prepare herself for middle-aged Robbie. However, unlike her own kitchen, there were just a few children's school photos still in their cardboard frames, along with yet more handicrafts, overwhelmingly goose and turkey-themed.

She glanced at her watch uneasily, thinking about her boiler repair.

'Will Robbie be long, do you think?' she asked when Lindy eventually returned, surprised to spot the hair freshly fluffed up, lip gloss reapplied, a cloud of flowery scent making her step back.

'We call him Bob.' The smile hardened. 'And he'll be as long as needs be. I told him not to come back until you and I have had a chat about something very precious and long overdue.'

'Is this about his grandmother's emerald ring?' Gill had a terrible suspicion it might be quite valuable.

Lindy stepped closer, deep voice low. 'This is about an apology, Gill.'

'Forgive me –' Before Gill could add *what apology are we talking about here exactly*, Lindy interrupted.

'Forgiven!' the toothy smile was firework bright once again. 'Glad we cleared that up.'

Realising Gill was too taken aback to speak, Lindy let out her sound barrier boom of a laugh. 'Your face!'

She laughed so much she had to wipe her eyes on a tea towel. 'Fact is Gill, if you'd bloody married Bob, it would have saved me thirty-five years of that moody lummock. And let's not even get started on his mother's bloody donkeys. Taking them away is the least you can do. Can you cut up that Victoria sponge for me?'

*

Petra perched on a sofa arm in fascination, observing Gill's daughters swoon as Travis gave them his killer smile and raked back his big mop of walnut curls to look from one to the other with his hypnotising eyes before asking in a husky voice. 'You're here about the donkeys?'

'That's right.' One sighed.

'Great granddad says you want to buy them?'

'Yes!' The other breathed.

'Loan one for an event this evening.' Petra corrected, feeling her smile stick, still wondering if she could adapt the panto costume in time.

'You know they're, like, all really *old*?'

'Really old?' Sighed the younger daughter, gazing into his eyes.

'Yeah,' he whispered back. 'Geriatric.'

Wishing modern teenagers had wittier repartee, like Richard Curtis movies or Wham lyrics, Petra casually asked him if he knew what any of their names were?

He flashed a swoon-making smile. 'Great Nana Betty gave them the same names over and over, I think. And she was, like, ancient, so I guess they have really *old* names?'

Sensing a touch of ageism, Petra asked chippily what classified as 'old' names: 'Ezekial? Jeremiah? Or Janet and John?' She stopped herself adding Karen just in time.

'Yeah, all those.'

'Simon, Lesley and Goldie?'

'Hilarious! *So* old!' They all laughed.

Feeling outdated, Petra felt her cheeks colour, looking round for distraction and admiring a tree hung with little padded stars made of hessian behind him. 'These are pretty.'

'Nan makes all the decorations. She sells them at Christmas markets.'

'I heard Lindy's quite the entrepreneur.'

'Yeah, she paints portraits too – that's one of hers,' he pointed out an oil hanging over the fireplace, 'Great granddad Ted and Nana Betty.'

What Petra had taken to be a repro print of a Renoir couple dancing was she now realised an original painted in its likeness featuring a tall, craggy figure in a flat cap spinning his small, round late wife in a bustled dress.

'And that's her and granddad Bob,' he pointed out Klimt's The Kiss reimagined with Robbie's white food prep hat and Lindy's wild hair. 'She sells loads on Etsy.

'Very talented woman,' Petra marvelled at their strangely appealing awfulness. 'Does she take commissions?' That would be Charlie's fiftieth sorted, the Gunns immortalised as Rubens' The Honeysuckle Bower.

'She and Grandad work all hours to pay for my school.' Travis swept a hand through the burnished curls again. '

'Where do you go?' asked one of the Walcote-Wish girls.

He named somewhere Petra had never heard of, explaining. 'It's a music school. It's kind of unique.'

'Can I go there for my A levels? I have grade seven flute.' Gill's other daughter sighed longingly.

'It's for kids with mobility issues and stuff.'

Petra noticed two crutches propped against his sofa arm, an oxygen cylinder discreetly tucked behind.

'I'm going to repay them when I'm a rock star.' He grinned, then coughed copiously, wheezing and spluttering.

'Are you okay?' Petra moved closer.

'Ashma.' He waved a dismissive hand. 'Pain in the backside.'

'He's our miracle!' Lindy marched back in with a steaming teapot, flanked by a pale-looking Gill with a tray of biscuits and pink-cheeked Aunt Evil with a sherry. 'Born at twenty-five weeks, was Travis. They gave him a fifty-fifty chance at best, but we're all or nothing in this family. That's one of his new songs, hey Travis?'

'*All or Nothing*.' Travis croaked with a big smile, eyes still streaming.

'Been used before, dear boy, or is yours a cover version?' Aunt Evil started humming the *Small Faces* hit, ignoring a discomfited Gill, shushing her under her breath. 'Raph and I partied at Steve Marriatt's Pimlico pad in sixty-six. *Such* a bad boy, but I did so like a bit of rough.' She eyed Travis mistily and started humming again.

'I don't know that one,' he looked worried.

'Oh, you must listen, it's...good grief!' Aunt Evil had caught sight of the fake Renoir over the fire, staring open-mouthed, her sentence unfinished.

'There are twenty different songs with the title *Call Me*,' Petra reassured Travis.

'Nobody calls anyone nowadays, Petra – we send voice notes,' Gill's younger daughter explained kindly.

'I call,' Travis said breezily, and both daughters agreed that maybe calling was making a come-back, like vinyl and wide-leg jeans. One asked him if they could hear his song.

He lowered his head, mop of hair covering his face modestly. 'You don't have to.'

'They bloody want to!' Lindy had dumped the teapot on the coffee table and picked up a remote to turn on the stereo in the corner. 'Play the song.'

'Oh yes, do!' Petra imagined someone as sensually cherubic would sound like a mixture between Styles and Bublé.

'If you're sure,' he took his phone and linked it to a cable trailing from the dusty stereo. 'This is my Christmas EP with All or Nothing on it. It's available on Soundcloud and Spotify.'

Moments later, they were all shaking under a deafening assault of low-fi drum'n'bass, looped samples and animal wailing.

Only Aunt Evil seemed oblivious, still staring dumbfounded at the reimagined Renoir.

Lindy started head-banging proudly, shouting. 'FANTASTIC, yah?'

'Amazing!' Petra marvelled at her lack of inhibition. Her musical taste rarely strayed from genres where you could make out the words of the lyrics these days.

She turned to Gill, who set down her tray so fast that the biscuits and cake slices bounced. Signalling for Petra to keep Lindy talking, Gill hurriedly pursued Aunt Evil, who was sidling back towards the kitchen, hands over her ears.

The girls were up on their feet with their hostess, all dancing around Petra. 'Come on, dance!

This is great! Merry Christmas!'

Closing her eyes, Petra tried hard to imagine she was back in the Elephant and Castle with a bandana and whistle in her Ministry of Sound Clubbing days.

And to her surprise, she stopped hearing nothing but noisy thumping and wails and started hearing jingle bells threading through bass riffs with a choir climbing arpeggios and reindeer bellowing while a drum thump-thump-thumped like Good King Wenceslas stomping through the snow. It was as rich and layered and complex as a slice of fruit-packed, brandy-soaked Christmas cake, and she loved it.

'I don't suppose you're available for a slot on New Year's Eve in Compton Magna Village Hall?' she bopped over to Travis.

*

'Put the sherry bottle down, Evelyn!' hissed Gill. 'You're incorrigible.'

'It's water,' Aunt Evil turned to her, gulping her way through her hydro flask before refilling it at the sink. 'I still feel a bit faint.'

'You should have stayed resting up in bed.' Gill told her, suspecting she'd be on a drip if she'd consumed as much sloe gin as her aunt last night.

'I am perfectly fine! It's just I thought he was dead.'

'Robbie?'

'No –' Aunt Evil's eyes widened.

Gill felt a blast of cold air as the outside door

was opened behind her.

'– him!'

Before Gill could turn, there was a metallic clatter as the hydro flask crashed to the ground, and then Aunt Evil fainted in her arms.

*

Eager to start donkey-dealing, Petra danced her way back to the kitchen where she found Gill man-handling her aunt's limp velour-clad body to a chair at the table where Evelyn groaned 'Ralph!' faintly and slumped over a colourful placemat with her head in her hands.

'What happened?' Petra rushed to help.

'He did.'

Framed in the kitchen door, stooping over his walking stick, was Ted Marlborough, blue eyes gleaming mischievously.

'Always had that effect on women,' he said, limping to an adjacent chair and nodding in passing at Petra. 'Hello again, angel.' He gave Gill a sterner look. 'You came, then.' Not waiting for a reply, he peered rheumily at Aunt Evil, who was blinking up at him through liver-spotted fingers. 'And who's this young lady? Have we met?'

'Don't pretend you don't remember,' sighed Aunt Evil, lowering her hands.

He closed one sparkling eye and cocked his chin. There was a long, expectant pause. Then he shook his head. 'Not a clue.'

Aunt Evil put her dark glasses back on huffily. 'Can someone please get a bloody donkey so we leave this place?'

'Gill must name one first,' Ted reminded her.

'How could I possibly know their names?' Gill protested crossly.

'The herd needs to go together,' Ted pronounced grandly. 'Robert promised his mother. All or nothing in this family.'

'I've only got a two-horse trailer,' Petra pointed out, glancing at the kitchen clock, 'and time is running out.'

'Best you talk to my Robert then.'

'That's your cue,' she gave Gill a prod.

Gill looked aghast. '*You* talk to him.'

Petra took her friend's hand and pulled her out into the porch that Ted had just come through, falling over his abandoned gumboots with an 'oof' before reminding Gill in an undertone. 'Robbie asked for you to come up here today specifically.'

'To tell him donkey names I've never heard of? It's a trap, Petra, don't you see? It's the Cambric shirt without any seams or needlework, the acre of land between the saltwater and the sea strand.'

'What has this to do with Simon and Garfunkel?'

'The song in an unrequited lover setting impossible tasks for the girl who rejected him. Like spinning straw into gold. Well, I'm not playing that game. I've already apologised to his wife. That's enough.'

'What did you apologise for?'

'I don't know exactly. She seemed to think I

ought to. Said it was my fault she married him.'

It struck Petra that Lindy, who worked tirelessly to keep the farm relevant and her house beautiful on a pittance thanks to her turbo-charged hippy energy – and possibly a few recreational drugs, she suspected – was doing much of the heavy lifting around here.

'Maybe Lindy's had enough of Rob– sorry, I mean 'Bob'?' She suggested brightly, eager for a positive spin to propel Gill donkey-wards. 'Just like you did at nineteen?'

Instead, Gill looked even more upset, whispering, 'I *hadn't* had enough of Robbie at nineteen! It was his mother, Betty, who made me end it.'

'His *mother*?' Petra gaped at her. 'Why?'

Glancing over her shoulder at the kitchen where Ted was helping himself and Aunt Evil to a sherry, Gill beckoned Petra outside, yet further away from earshot.

'Betty told me there was no future in it, that I had to break it off for all our sakes.'

Petra's mind instantly raced with wild ideas recycled from her fictional plots: perhaps Betty Marlborough and Henry Walcote had enjoyed a tumultuous affair, and Gill and Robbie were half-siblings? Or had Robbie been secretly betrothed to Lindy since infancy for the sake of the family's farming dynasty? Or was Betty a jealous monster who loathed Gill's youthful beauty? 'What reason did she give?'

'She told me Robbie was unhappy, but he didn't know how to end it...' Gill grimaced and looked away, battling emotion.

Petra, who wasn't accustomed to seeing her friend anything other than calm, cynical and in control, was thrown. The first flakes of snow were starting to fall, tiny cool prickles against her face. 'Did you always do what his mother told you to?'

'Of course not! But I already knew...I'd guessed...that I wasn't what Robbie was really looking for. We rushed into it. We wanted different things. I was a total swot, for a start, and he was such a catch.'

'You, my brilliant, clever, beautiful, kind friend, are the rare, rainbow-scaled one that got away. You're *wonderful*.'

'Save the hyperbole for your books,' Gill scoffed, embarrassed pink stains on her cheeks, but she looked secretly bucked up.

'Does Robbie know that's the reason you broke it off?' Petra asked, then seeing Gill give a dismissive shrug, she added: 'Because if he doesn't, this might be the moment to put things straight.'

'He vowed he'd never speak to me again.'

'You'll be the one doing the talking.'

Gill looked doubtful, snow landing in her furled eyebrows. 'Why rake it all up again now?'

'Because he asked you to come here. And because it's Christmas.'

To Petra's surprise, she took the cue, muttering, 'You're right!' and marching off down the garden path.

'Good luck!' Petra called after her. 'And don't forget –'

'To ask for a donkey, I know!'

'How wonderful you are!' Petra corrected.

*

Gill was surprised how little changed the Broad Compton Farm buildings remained from how she remembered them. They were old fashioned and meticulously preserved with endless careful patching, the same vintage Massey Ferguson parked in the yard alongside a newer quad bike.

Robbie was nowhere to be seen, but the donkeys still lived in the little paddock alongside the open barn. About ten were huddled around a metal hay feeder, snow speckling their thick coats. They looked a contented bunch.

She could still vividly picture Betty carrying a whole haybale, fingers reddening beneath the twine, laughing and talking to them as they crowded around her. What had she named them? Gill had a feeling there was a theme.

She stood by the rails watching them, wondering at their 'wild' reputation. Betty had bred for temperament. She'd joke self-deprecatingly that she was daft as a donkey, which was why she liked them, whereas Gill was fleet-footed as the horses she loved, but that they were both stubborn as mules.

Kind, motherly Betty had always treated Gill like one of her daughters, bolstering her confidence by telling her how brave and strong she was.

It was up here at the farm that Betty had begged her to let Robbie go. Gill had accepted a last-minute invitation to lunch the same day as the Compton Magna carol-singing procession. It was two days before Christmas, another Sunday like this. The anniversary wasn't lost on her.

Dressed in her full piecrust and pearls, she'd rattled into the farmyard in her Mini Metro expecting the usual big Marlborough family roast with Ted, Robbie and his sisters all there. But it had just been Betty offering a mug of strong red Tetleys and a mince pie, eyes red from crying. The others were visiting Ted's sister and her family over Evesham way, she'd explained.

Betty wasn't a woman of many words or high emotion. But that day, there had been no stopping her tears.

'I can't let him do it anymore, Gill!' She'd wailed. 'This has to stop, do you hear? He's too precious. I can't lose him. You have to put a stop to it, Gill, for everyone's sake!'

Betty had spoken with such breathless, panic-stricken speed that Gill had barely got a word in edgeways, but the message had been clear enough. Robbie needed a way out.

'He don't want any of this, wishes he'd never got muddled up in it all, but he's no idea how to make it stop. Can't you see, he's in way over his head? It was never supposed to go this far.'

'Has he told you this?'

'We both know that man would rather cut his

off a finger than show emotion. But I'll tell you this and no one else: I've had him weeping in my lap more than once over this. It breaks my heart to see him like that. I need you to help me, Gill. We're stronger than they are. Sometimes, we have to be the ones to act. You must help him for all our sakes. Put a stop to it, do you hear?'

Gill belonged to a generation brought up not to question their elders, certainly not a parent about a child. Certainly not doughty, salt-of-the-earth Betty Marlborough, who never lied, manipulated or played games, and was the polar opposite of her own family.

There was another reason she hadn't questioned the devastating news. Because there, laid bare, was the unspoken truth she'd suspected all along, a niggling self-doubt that handsome, rugged Robbie Marlborough could never really want to marry her. He had only asked her because he thought that would lead to bed, and as soon as she made it clear she wanted to wait longer, he'd secretly wanted out.

'It's just animal instinct with men.' Betty had confirmed her fears, words coming out so quickly she was like a vinyl album played at 45rpm. 'They get tunnel vision with wanting a woman, never think of the consequences, especially when she makes herself...available. He thought it was there for the taking, but marriage is a sacred thing, Gill, it's far more than just...the act.'

That had cut deep. *He thought it was there for*

the taking. The lump in Gill's throat had made it impossible to speak, as Betty told her: 'You mustn't breathe a word of this conversation. Marlborough men are so proud. But we can't let it carry on, can we?'

A squelching and snuffling snapped her back to the present. The donkeys had come over to see who was standing by their gate and whether they had any food. With their turned-down triangular eyes and quiet determination, they reminded Gill of Betty Marlborough.

She'd shown unwavering, determined loyalty that awful afternoon, telling Gill: 'It breaks my heart to see him this miserable. He told me he couldn't face another Christmas with things like they are. Even threatened to blow his brains out.'

The thought had made Gill feel physically sick, her head light, bile rising.

'Silly fool keeps hoping it'll just go away,' Betty had rushed on. 'He's too weak to call it off himself. Typical man. Like I say, we women are stronger. We'll stand up and say it like it is while a man will just put two barrels in his mouth and be done.'

Gill had made up her mind at that moment to break off the engagement, for all their sakes but above all for Robbie.

She did it that evening, as soon as she could get him alone. Waiting through the nativity procession had been agony, the knowledge of what lay ahead making her throat too dry to sing, her heart too heavy to look at him. When she finally did it, she'd made it as quick and pragmatic as possible. She'd blamed her studies, her ambition, and her own change of heart with no mention of his. She'd left no space for argument.

It remained amongst the single most painful experiences in her life, up there with childbirth, grief, bones breaking and a long career in which cruelty and tragedy constantly give the lie to man's love of animals. Like her late Aunt Vile, Gill had always secretly preferred animals to people.

'It's all animal instinct with men!'

The thing was, Gill liked men, too. After twenty-eight years as Paul's wife, she knew marriage was about anything but sex most of the time. She sometimes wished that side was a bit livelier, but Paul had always been quite passive on that front. She was also occasionally guilty of wondering if it would have been different with Robbie, whose kisses had once made her entire body bubble through like a Soda Stream. And now she was guilty of playing *What If* with that awful day she'd broken it off, wishing she hadn't run away before giving him a chance to reply. She'd proved a creature of flight, just as Betty always said. Gill knew Betty would understand why she had succumbed to her own animal instincts and fled, fearing more pain inflicted on both sides. But she and Betty had never spoken again, either.

A warm donkey muzzle was pressed against her hand through the gate's bars, nuzzling for treats. Gill stroked it, scratching the heavy jowls and the broad forehead. What *was* it Betty had named them all after?

The snowfall had started to thicken, white clumps gathering on the little herd's coats and ear tufts. She let herself in with them, and they crowded around, nosing at her pockets, breaths clouding in little dragon puffs, warm and companionable. 'You're no wilder than I am.'

A throat clearing behind her made them skitter away, and Gill spun around.

Robbie was leaning over the gate. Impossibly tall and broad in a long stock coat, scarves and hat, he looked like an Edwardian polar explorer. Her heart felt like it had stopped. What shocked her was how much he resembled his father at that age.

She opened her mouth to say hello, remembered the silence pact and closed it again. Let Robbie speak first.

With his coattails swinging, he climbed over the gate, still able to hurdle five bars in two steps.

The donkeys surged forward again, crowding around him, recognising a regular food source. Gill was soon cast adrift amid a sea of brown, hairy, sweet-smelling greed. Robbie rowed his way towards her, coming to a halt two donkeys away.

Still they didn't speak, a curious pas de deux amongst the bustling, territorial herd.

All or nothing, Gill remembered the unofficial Marlborough family motto.

She reached into her pocket and pulled out his grandmother's emerald ring.

Handing it back would be the big gesture they both needed, she'd realised, her downpayment on redemption, drawing a line, moving on, breaking the silence. They were three times the age they had been, were both now married and parents – grandparent in his case – who should at least be able to say hello civilly.

But as she held the ring out to him, jostled by the herd, it dropped from her grip and disappeared beneath half a dozen donkeys.

*

Ted was flirtily trying to ply Petra with sherry. 'Have one of these, and I'll tell you the one about the time I stopped a cock fight in Bagot Woods.'

'I'm driving, I really can't,' she apologised, having already heard the one about the poultry shed fire he'd fought single-handedly and the gun-toting poachers he'd brought down.

'I'll have hers!' Evelyn presented her empty schooner.

In the sitting room, Travis Marlborough's Christmas trance anthems thudded on repeat, the teenagers happily chatting over it, cats bolstering the sofa backs and windowsills.

When Petra popped her head round the door, Lindy was still goth dancing like a Blitz Club regular, lost to her grandson's music. She was an incongruous farmer's wife, this larger-than-life force of nature. She wasn't the only big personality here.

In the kitchen behind her, Aunt Evil was glaring

at Ted Marlborough over her dark glasses in a way Petra found professionally fascinating. It was a Jocasta to Oedipus, Alexis to Blake, Nicole to Tom.

'I'd quite forgotten you were what Heinous called the "farmer-in-law". Must have blanked it.'

'Should I know you?' he asked again affably.

'You ended my marriage, Ted. Or rather, we did.'

*

The snow fell thickly as Gill and Robbie scrabbled beneath the shifting, snorting donkeys searching for the dropped emerald ring. Soon, they could barely see. Gill was trodden on twice, her hand trampled, but she gritted her teeth and said nothing as her fingers dug and raked the muddy grass, occasionally crossing with his.

It was slippy underfoot, the donkeys refusing to stay away no matter how many times Robbie clapped his hands to shoo them off, or Gill pulled off her woolly hat to wave it above her head. She was wary of the little herd, which might not be as wild as Petra had suggested but was getting more excitable by the minute with the snow thickening and humans behaving like dogs underfoot. Yet Robbie knew them well and seemed unbothered, shouldering them away like toddlers, a wry half-smile on his face. They just wanted to join in the fun, bustling back, eager to help.

Gill wasn't sure at what point they started to laugh, but suddenly, the absurdity of the situation – and the timing – was just too much. It was the oddest feeling, regressing forty years to the unstoppable giggles she'd forgotten they'd once shared.

And it was impossible to stay silent. Irrepressible laughter had no mute switch.

Gulping and hooting, she knelt in the white-dusted mud. Robbie crouched nearby, forearms on his knees and hiccoughed through uncontainable mirth, surrounded by donkeys.

*

Ted Marlborough was staying remarkably calm for a man accused of marriage-wrecking. In fact, Petra sensed something about the earthy smile he was giving Aunt Evil that suggested this wasn't entirely unfamiliar territory.

Evelyn had missile-locked him in her femme fatale glare again. 'When my husband Ralph found out about us, he told me it was over.'

'You'll need to jog my memory, Mrs.'

Evelyn sighed impatiently. 'Cast your mind back to the late seventies: an after-show-party, curly blonde hair and a velvet jumpsuit. You told me I looked like Petula Clarke, topped up my Mateus Rose once too often, and we kissed under the mistletoe.'

'I was a smooth operator in those days.' He looked chuffed at the thought,

'The following year, we met again, carol singing on the Green. I was in a Biba sheepskin coat and Mary Quant knee boots; we shared a hipflask and a stolen moment behind a horse chestnut. Your wife took you home early.'

'Very jealous woman, Betty. Always giving me

an earful for getting frisky with young ladies, but I only did it when I was too bevvied to know better or remember afterwards.' He topped up their sherries with a game look.

Aunt Evelyn gave him a critical one in return, not buying the amnesia line. 'We were both... in our cups, Ted. And I remember very well how determined you were. And how handsome. A year later, we met again at the Christmas Concert in the village hall. I was wearing the most divine Oscar de la Renta trouser suit. The after-party was raucous, and we took some fresh air together. Your wife caught us embracing by Santa's sleigh.'

Ted gazed into his sherry schooner with a deep sigh. 'What can I say? Betty knew I was a weak man, but I loved her. I'm sorry to say it happened more than once. Always had to throw myself at her mercy, offer to fall on my sword.'

'Yes, well, your sword obviously wasn't sharp enough because she came to see me in person. She was distraught. Apparently, she'd asked Gill to warn me to leave you alone and say you wanted out, but then she and that boy of yours had their big tiff and split up, so Betty drove down to Compton Magna to do it herself and was *very* accusatory. She called *me* a flirt for leading you on! My brother's family were all out hunting, but my husband was in the next room.' She reached for her flask, unscrewing its top with shaking hands, 'and he overheard everything.'

'Betty knew it was only a bit of festive fun.'

'That's what I told Ralph, but it was the straw

that broke the camel's back. He walked out on me a week later.'

'Over a little Christmas slap and tickle?' Ted scoffed.

'There had been other – indiscretions. It's why we'd come home from Hong Kong. Expat life can be very louche; all the booze and boredom.' She lifted the sherry glass and put it down again. 'I just wanted to cheer myself up, make him jealous. He was so terribly dry, my husband. And Christmas is all about having fun, isn't it?'

Not if you break off your engagement two days before it, thought Petra. Nor if that break-up comes out of the blue. And not if you only do it because you believe you're sparing the one you love pain, gifting them the freedom they crave, sacrificing your own happiness to save them.

Her mind was on overdrive once more. She remembered Gill saying *Betty told me there was no future in it, that I had to break it off for all our sakes.*

Had Betty really meant to end her son's engagement as Gill imagined, Petra wondered. Or had she simply wanted to put a stop to her own husband's flirtation with Aunt Evil: *she'd asked Gill to warn me to leave you alone and say you wanted out.*

Oh, heck.

'I might just pop outside for some fresh air.' She hurried towards the porch.

*

The snow had slowed Gill and Robbie's search for the dropped ring, fits of laughter impeding it further.

Yet both kept coming thick and fast.

When they finally saw it glitter, neatly impressed into the mud on one elderly donkey's fetlock like a wedding page's cushion, it set them off again.

Gill regained enough self-control to peel it off and hand it to him.

'Thank you.'

Was the curse broken as simply as that, she wondered? His voice was deeper than she remembered, hanging in the air like an echo.

'Sorry I kept it so long.'

They laughed again, less explosive this time, more relieved.

The donkeys were still crowding in jealously, overexcited by this rare human company. One let out a furious squeal as another bit it, rear end spinning round like a tank gun to aim a kick.

Gill realised a split-second too late that she would be in the way as it double-barrelled its adversary. Before she could react, Robbie had dived forward between her and the hooves. Surprise lit up his face as he was caught in the crossfire, sent off balance by the first hoof clipping his shoulder, followed a millisecond later by another clouting his temple with an audible smack. He slumped sideways.

'Oh bloody hell,' Gill lunged forward to catch him, pulling him with effort from the donkey scrum. Then, for the second time in an hour, she lugged a semi-conscious body towards a quiet spot to recover.

*

'Gill!' Petra marched alongside the donkey paddock, the snow flurrying down so thickly she could barely see a thing. But she could hear the herd, squealing, hee-hawing and stamping, clearly wound up.

Perhaps the carol singing processions would be cancelled, she wondered hopefully, checking her phone.

Several urgent messages greeted her from Auriol Bullock, insisting that the show must go on and demanding to know whether she should raid the CADS costume store for the two-man cow suit? *Rev v keen on having real thing, but both worried poo could be a Health and Safety issue with small people. AB*

Suspecting poo was less of an issue than gnashing teeth and flying hooves, Petra peered warily in the direction of the snow-caked donkey herd, which she could now just make out bustling for shelter beneath the overhang of an open barn, the squeals gradually subsiding as each found a slot and they shared body warmth. Surely one of them could be won over by carrots and cuddles? The cow costume was hideous. And it had *udders*.

She thought she spotted someone moving further inside the barn. 'Hello? Gill!'

There was no reply. When she let herself in the gate, the donkeys turned and started gambolling towards her like abominable snow beasts, bucking and bouncing against one another in their haste.

Petra hurriedly backed out, deciding it might be a better idea to get help.

First, she fired back a quick message to Auriol: *Agree Donkey poo highly toxic. Might need COSHH form/indemnity. Will investigate. Petra. Ps) Do we still have the camel suit from Aladdin?*

*

Propped up on some hay bales behind sheep hurdling, Robbie groaned and rubbed his head. 'What happened?'

'You were seeing stars.'

'I saw *you*,' he muttered, eyeing her in the gloom. 'Didn't think you'd ever come up here again.'

'Petra hijacked me. She is desperate for a donkey. Said you'd told her I had to name one like a ruddy Disney quest.'

He half-laughed, looking away. 'I'd had a drink.'

'And then your wife told me she wanted to meet me.'

He sucked away the smile. 'That too.'

'She's not at all how I'd imagined.'

His gaze held hers, eyes always at their greenest when challenging. 'What did you imagine?'

Somebody old-fashioned and straitlaced like his mother – like Gill herself – but she wasn't going to say that. She stuck to plain truths. 'I like her.'

'Been together a long time,' he looked away. 'Lindy was eighteen when we wed; I wasn't yet twenty-one and thought it might stop me missing you.'

His openness made Gill uncomfortable,

swallowing a flint-like lump in her throat. 'Did it?'

'She's one hell of a woman. Kept this place going.' His gaze moved around the barn, and then he smiled at the half dozen pairs of eyes watching them over the sheep hurdles. 'Not so keen on donkeys. Thinks my mum lives on through them.'

'Seriously?'

'She's full of all this reincarnation stuff, is Lindy. She was a vegan when we met. Mum thought we were mad, wanting to get wed, kept telling me to go after you, sort things out. But you were overseas.'

'Still on my gap year in Borneo,' she realised.

He nodded. 'Then Lindy fell pregnant, so we brought the wedding forward, and Mum said no more about it for years.'

'And now you're a grandfather as well as a dad?'

'Two daughters, and a son, and four grandchildren so far. Our boy and his family live over in South Africa; our oldest girl is in Wales with hers. We lost their kid sister to leukaemia at eighteen, but you know that.'

'I don't know anything, I'm afraid.'

'It's her boy who lives with us, Travis. Never knew his mum. She lives on through him.'

Gill thought back to the pretty teenager Lindy had brought to anti-natal appointments. 'I've just met him, a talented musician.'

'He's no farmer, that's for sure,' he rubbed the sad smile from his mouth, then raked back his peppery hair, feeling for the bump and wincing. Then he reached into his pocket to check he still had the ring, pulling it out with relief.

He wiped it on his sleeve. 'I'd forgotten you still had this.'

'Seriously?'

'I prefer to forget most of what happened, to be honest.'

She nodded, 'Me too.'

'Who am I kidding? That was a lie. I think about it every Christmas.'

'Same here.'

This time, the laughter didn't take hold.

He gave her a sad, sideways smile, a sparkle in his eyes that she didn't remember being there at nineteen. 'You worked out any of their names then, the donkeys?'

'How am I supposed to do that?'

'You're the clever one.' He eyed her shrewdly. 'Mum named them all.'

Gill raked back through her mind to try to recall Betty's herd forty years ago, grand-sires and grand-dams to these. She still had a vivid memory of her shouting and rattling a bucket, small and steadfast in a khaki Husky jacket. Hadn't there been a Bert named after Ted's late father? Two Berts, in fact. And Nellie and Joan after far-flung school friends. The donkeys had been named after absent loved ones, she remembered at last, Betty's auld acquaintances. There had even been a Skipper after a beloved childhood sheepdog.

If this was a cruel practical joke at her expense, she might as well take the bow, she realised. 'Okay, tell me which one is Gill?'

Laughing, Robbie clapped his big hands together in applause. 'You always were a bright spark.'

Then he stood up and started along the line of faces watching them, introducing each in turn, beginning with a buff brown alpha with an eager expression. '*This* is Gill, and here's Henry...' He was soon reeling off familiar names: her mother and maternal grandparents, Aunt Violet, Gill's three daughters and even their father, who was fittingly small and cross-looking.

'They're *all* named after my family?' she realised in shock.

'Mum never forgave herself for what happened between us, or me for not fighting to hold onto you. She missed you all, the Walcotes, missed knowing you.'

'But Betty was the one who told me to end it. She said that you were unhappy.'

He looked away, half-smiling. 'I wasn't unhappy, Gill. *You* were.'

'That's not true! I regretted it the moment I said it. I tried to drive up to see you that night, but the snow was too thick.'

'It melted eventually; I don't know if you noticed.'

'I wanted to call, to write. But I kept bottling it. I thought I'd just make it worse, saying I'd been wrong, asking you to reconsider. Your mother had told me you couldn't pluck up the courage to end it.'

'Are you sure Mum was talking about us?'

Gill tried to make sense of this, looking at the snow-backed donkeys staring at her with Betty's kind eyes and her family's names. 'If not us, then who *was* she talking about?'

'Does it matter? Fact is, you'd heard what you needed. And you were right: we wanted different things in life; you had to put your studies first. I knew you meant every word you said.'

'Then you knew me better than I knew myself.'

He looked at the ring again, turning it round in his big, calloused fingers: 'Mum was happy for you when you married that vet. She cut out the announcement in the paper. "It's the right way of things, Robert," she said. Knew you'd find yourself a good man to love.'

She nodded, biting her inner lip hard.

'And did you?' The sparkle was back in his eyes, oddly familiar.

'I did.' She found herself gazing at her husband's asinine namesake, a small, handsome black donkey Betty Marlborough had named after a man she'd never met. Paul Wish, who couldn't talk to his wife about his feelings at all. Did he confide in their bubbly practice nurse instead? *Methinks I was enamoured of an ass.*

'And you found somebody to love too,' she said eventually.

'Found her,' Robbie agreed. There was a long pause. 'Then lost her.'

Gill watched the snow floating down, flakes as

fat as confetti.

In the shared silence that followed, she guessed Robbie might be in a similar place to her, at the thin end of a tricky and uncommunicative marriage. Mourning lost love.

She couldn't look at him, but she knew he was watching her.

'Mum had to fight for her marriage,' he said eventually. 'Dad was a devil for a pretty face, still is. Used to get drunk every Christmas and do silly stuff that drove her half mad.'

'What silly stuff?' Gill had visions of Ted, caned on Tia Maria, leering at a Benny Hill special.

'This.' He stooped to plant a kiss on her lips.

She reeled back. 'What was that for?'

'Don't tell me this isn't still nineteen-eighty?' his eyes sparkled even brighter, voice fathoms deep. 'Have I had a bump on my head or something?'

A shout from the gate sent the donkeys bucking away, and Gill turned to see Petra retreating at speed from the waist-height stampede.

Then she saw Lindy marching through them like Moses parting the Red Sea, her fierce face thunderous.

'Oh hell.' Robbie muttered as Lindy hurdled the barrier with a war cry and aimed a punch.

Gill's reaction was pure kneejerk, she would later realise. The fact her head and her heart were telling her entirely different things was irrelevant. Some strange cortex-deep sense of fairness instantly alerted her unconscious mind that Robbie had saved her from a donkey kick earlier, meaning it was only fair to return the favour.

And as donkeys scattered and she screamed 'Noooooooo!' she knew that Betty Marlborough had been right.

It all came down to animal instinct.

*

'I can't believe they had no frozen peas!' Petra lamented as she drove back towards Compton Magna. 'No frozen veg or fruit of any description.'

'It's fine,' Gill insisted.

'You think they'd have cranberries.'

'Honestly, this is perfect,' the reply came through gritted teeth, as Gill pressed a bag of frozen turkey giblets to her eye.

'She has a mean right hook, that Lindy.'

'Telling me.'

They lapsed into silence for a while, Petra focussing on navigating the narrow, snowy lane. It had stopped falling at least, the heavy clouds lumbering south to white-out Gloucestershire and Oxfordshire for Instagram-ready Christmases. Behind them, Aunt Evil was asleep, Gill's daughters both earplugged, phones aloft, heads bobbing as they listened to Travis Marlborough's playlist on Spotify, matching new crushes being cherished.

'Sorry about the donkey,' Gill said eventually.

'It's fine. Auriol is sewing ears on a panto cow suit as we speak.'

'I *did* name one correctly.' She said competitively.

'Well done.'

Petra wouldn't dream of saying anything about the kiss while Gill's loved ones were in the car, even though they wouldn't overhear a thing. She wasn't sure she was ever going to mention it. The shock of seeing her friend in a clinch with the Daniel Craig of the Bardswolds still resonated. Gill was usually so unimpeachable, upright, up*tight*. Petra would never have brought her along today if she'd thought this would happen. Infuriatingly, she was also slightly jealous.

But Gill was too eager to clear her name for discretion, stage whispering. 'I did nothing to encourage it, you know that.'

'Of course.'

'He's turning into his father. I knew I recognised that twinkle in his eye. Ted has always been an opportunist. Betty worried Robbie would turn out just the same. Thank god I didn't marry him. No wonder Lindy defends her territory so fiercely. Poor Betty didn't have that privilege.'

Awash with relief, Petra was ashamed of herself for doubting her friend's moral fibre. Her own was far weaker: 'Good job she warned you off, eh?'

The giblets were lowered, and Gill turned to face her. 'Or did she?'

Then she whispered urgently: 'What if Betty was talking about one of Ted's dalliances she wanted me to put an end to?'

'What makes you think that?' Petra asked lightly, glancing in her rearview mirror at sleeping

Aunt Evil.

Gill might only have one functioning eye, but Petra could tell it was watching her closely. 'Something Robbie said.'

Under scrutiny, Petra wrinkled her nose and hummed ambiguously.

'Betty used to tell me I was much braver than her and could put things into words she couldn't. "Articulated", she called it.'

'That's strangely Freudian.' Petra glanced at the mirror again, double-checking Aunt Evil was definitely asleep. 'Strong, flexible, capable of taking heavy loads.'

'And did you know she named all her donkeys after me and my family, even Paul and our children?'

'Less kind perhaps.'

'It was meant as an honour.'

'Still, donkeys aren't known for their intelligence, are they?'

The giblets went back up, and Gill turned away huffily. Then, after a pause, she whispered. 'I think perhaps I have made a stupid mistake.'

Petra glanced across in alarm. 'Stupid how?'

Gill and the giblets turned back. 'I was a lot more articulated when I was with Robbie. I really miss that...articulation.'

'We're none of us as flexible over forty,' Petra said vaguely, not liking the way Gill's good eye was developing a preoccupied, dreamy look.

In fact, it was starting to twinkle.

PART FOUR

The boiler engineer was hard at work when Gill got home, an infuriated Paul forced to come back from the clinic early to let him in. 'You said you'd be back by eleven! I messaged twice.'

'Sorry, just call me another time,' she hurried past him, hoping he didn't notice her blackening eye.

Gill was covering that afternoon's practice work, rushing back outside first to bring her horse in from the snow, then grabbing a bag of crisps as lunch. Thank goodness Aunt Evil retired straight to bed for a siesta with her electric blanket at max, the girls heading to the Gunns' underfloor-heated kitchen to plot something with Petra's teenage sons. Gill left Paul lecturing the engineer about renewables whilst checking his phone messages, not bothering to say goodbye.

'You need to be more articulated!' she told herself crossly in the rearview mirror as she drove through the snow, sparkling salt white under a cold winter sun now, fittingly Arctic. Her bruised eye didn't look too bad, she realised with relief, a thumbprint-sized red patch forming beneath that blended into the tiredness dark circles already there. She fished some dark glasses from the glove box, then realised she looked like Aunt Evil had earlier. Her dissipated future beckoned.

Lindy hadn't meant to hit Gill at all, of course. She hadn't even intended to hit Robbie, she'd insisted afterwards, apologising profusely and explaining that she'd been going for the maddened double fist-shake 'not again!' screaming confrontation with her husband. Gill admired her tenacity.

Like Betty before her, Lindy Marlborough had to fight for her marriage. Unlike Betty, she had a considerable armoury: self-confidence, business acumen, physical power, creativity and a suspicious mind. Plus one hell of a punch.

The bad weather had brought the usual flurry of emergency calls, but Gill was grateful to be kept busy all afternoon, her mind forced to stay on task. Navigating the snow in the 4x4, she scoped, scanned and stitched, checked digital pulses and dug out abscesses, lifted by the Christmas cheer, by the mince pies and Quality Street, lights in trees and bottles of thank you wine. To her frustration, her eye swelled and blackened beneath the dark glasses, commented on each time a practical task forced her to remove them. She joked it off as a headbutt from a donkey.

In truth, it was her heart that was far more bruised.

Back at the clinic, she checked around the inpatients one-eyed, assisted by the veterinary nurse she knew her husband secretly messaged. 'Crikey, Gill, what happened to you?'

'I'm training to be a cage fighter, didn't Paul say? You should see my opponent. No teeth left!' It bucked her up briefly. But it was far from "articulated".

Home by five, Gill went straight to the stable yard where a rapturous fanfare of wickers and whinnies welcomed her and she spent too long feeding and fussing, skipping out and changing rugs. This was when she felt most loved and needed nowadays. Once again, she mourned the busy days of the girls having ponies, the excited chatter and Christmas songs on the yard radio. She let her mind drift back to the days Paul still rode, keeping an ex-racer here he'd team-chased and drag-hunted. When first married, they'd ridden out together at every opportunity, long before she'd joined the Bags to spend hours on horseback complaining about their husbands.

Inside at last, the house was warming up again, although the welcome felt predictably frosty, the dogs whining out of sight. Donning her dark glasses, she tracked them down to Paul's office, where they body wagged and flopped down to offer bellies to be rubbed, trapping her ankles.

Her husband was talking on his phone, ringing off and pocketing it when she walked in.

He cleared his throat grouchily, headmaster-like. 'Everything okay?'

'Fine. And here?' She fell over a dog and was forced to remove her shades, turning her good side to him.

'I'd have messaged if it wasn't,' he pretended to read something on his computer screen, adding pointedly, 'or *called* you' to show he'd been listening earlier.

Gill remembered her daughter saying nobody did that anymore. Except that Paul had just been on a call. She wanted to ask who he'd been speaking with, but that would sound paranoid.

Instead, she quoted Petra. 'Did you know there are twenty different songs with the title *Call Me*?'

Paul glanced up at her as if she was mad. She could feel her black eye twitching, the normal cheery brusqueness of her voice surprising her. 'Don't forget the carol singing this evening! We need to be on the Green in an hour. The girls are at Petra's. Aunt Evil is still in her room, I take it?'

'Must be,' he was reading his screen again.

When Gill took Evelyn a cup of tea, her aunt was buried entirely under her many fleece throws and duvets, so deeply asleep she had a brief panic she might have expired until a voice beneath the layers grumbled: 'The only T that I drink at this hour has a G in it, darling – now fetch me one of those,' and a hand popped out to shoo her away. Then she cried: 'Wait!'

Almost out of the door, Gill waited.

Aunt Evil's pink face popped out, thin blonde hair on end like a baby eagle chick. 'Don't make the same mistakes as me, darling! Fell into dishy Ted Marlborough's arms three years running to make Ralph jealous. Never worked. Always felt wretched about it afterwards. Bally good kisser, mind you. Can I have cucumber instead of lemon in my gin?'

On the landing, Gill slotted this revelation into the gaps in her memory. She'd as good as guessed it. Evelyn and Ted. It had even been captured on the Super 8, the jiving mutual attraction, those wayward Christmas party rules of yesteryear. Yet the brutal truth of it still winded her because of everything it ransacked. When Betty had asked Gill to help put an end to her aunt's flirtation, she'd misunderstood horribly. Or had she? Perhaps Robbie was right; perhaps Gill had heard what she wanted to, grateful for an excuse to run away, to broaden her horizons, and find a love based on minds as well as hearts.

Except those minds had built separate fortresses, their hearts vaulted inside, even with the Christmas decorations up.

She had to talk to Paul, she realised. She had to be "articulated".

Gill's phone started ringing as she made her way downstairs, a mobile number she didn't recognise. Guessing it was another veterinary emergency – they were almost the only calls she ever got, her daughter was right – she paused halfway down to take it.

The line was terrible, breaking up too much to make out more than fractions of words 'Ear...hell...

ill!'

Gill moved back up to find a better signal. 'I'm sorry, who did you say?'

'It's Rob–' the deep voice stuttered, and she gripped the banister to stop herself falling. Then it came back more clearly: 'It's Bob's wife Lindy here, hello? Can you hear me? Is that Gill?'

'Yes, I can hear you,' she braced herself for a verbal assault, still gripping the banister.

Instead, she heard the big burst of drumroll laughter. 'Don't hang up, love. It's my turn to apologise.'

'I didn't –'

'Bob's told me what his Mum did,' Lindy interrupted, her voice starting to echo, 'and I've left him –' They were abruptly cut off.

*

'I can't wear these ears. They keep slipping,' moaned the muffled voice in the front end of the donkey.

'Of course you can!' Petra told her husband. 'You have the better end of the deal, trust me. What *are* these trousers you're wearing underneath here?'

'Tartan bondage. Bought them off eBay. Rather fun, I thought. Plan to pogo at the afterparty back here later. Damn, the ears have slipped again.'

Petra wriggled out from beneath the fabric cow-donkey back, hot-faced and furious. '*What* afterparty back here?'

Charlie's colossal cow head turned towards her, fluffy ears pointing out front like Minotaur horns. 'Didn't I say? The boys are setting it up for us.

Theme: Punk Christmas.'

Petra's teenage sons were two wannabe party promoters, cheerfully egged on by their sociable father, who still dreamed of owning an Ibiza nightclub. 'How many?'

'The carol singers, a couple of village WhatsApp groups, cricket team, a few mates from the Jugged Hare. And the boys are inviting some chums, with the Walcote-Wish girls asking friends along to help up the female quota. I said no more than twenty teenagers.'

Which Petra knew meant forty, snow or no snow. 'Have you forgotten your mother's due here first thing tomorrow?'

'Hoping I might if I drink enough later, haha!' The laugh turned to a heehaw donkey bray. He readjusted his ears and held up the tail end of his costume invitingly. 'Climb aboard. Let's arse around. Need to get going soon, and we haven't practised the walk.'

Petra didn't budge, crossing her arms, asking through gritted teeth. 'Who exactly is going to clear up after this party?'

'I'll lend a hand. I'm sure the kids can help, too. And what about our pretty char, can she come round?' His ears slipped again, now yak-like.

'It's Christmas Eve tomorrow, Charlie!'

'In that case, sorry, count me out. Need to go out and buy you a pressie. Are you getting back in this thing, Petra darling? Darling, what are you doing to my ears?"

Gripping one in each hand, she tugged off his head. 'I've always been the eyes and ears of our marriage, Charlie, so I'm going to be the front end of this donkey. We're swapping! You've been demoted, darling. Now bend over and take it like a man, you punk.'

*

Sitting in front of her dressing table, Gill covered the bruised, puffy skin around her right eye with her only bottle of foundation, which owed its optimistic shade more to summer tan than winter pallor. She hated wearing makeup but wanted it gone, this reminder of her twisted, mistaken nostalgia. Especially now that it also served as a reminder of what she'd just done to the Marlboroughs' marriage. She could hardly blame Lindy for making a stand. Betty had been right: *We're stronger than they are. Sometimes, we have to be the ones to act.* At nineteen, Gill had been strong; at almost sixty, she was less so.

But this evening, she could feel a renewed life force pumping through her veins. History was repeating itself.

Paul was in the shower, the pipes humming, the radio playing Christmas hits on a cheesy channel pretending everybody's having fun, rocking around Frosty the Snowman on a happy holiday.

She should wait until after the village carol procession. Duty dictated it.

Staring at her middle-aged reflection, Gill steeled herself to put on the Walcote-Wish show, saddened that they would be the family's sole representatives. The girls had messaged that they were too busy helping the Gunn boys set up a 'happening vibe'. Aunt Evil was still in bed with her G&T, insisting she wanted to catch up with the soaps on her tablet.

She glanced over her shoulder at her own bed enviously, yawns pulling at her jowls, too many nights of insomnia catching up with her. Then she caught a flash of hairy chest and thigh, along with a glimpse of a lowering red towel and hurriedly turned back to the mirror. These days, studying her husband's body for too long felt like an intrusion. She did it even less than he looked her in the face.

Gill caught her own eye in the mirror, the truth hurting. The orange foundation around her eye made her look like a hound with a tan patch. This evening, if she painted her face with a dog's nose and whiskers, Paul would probably be none the wiser until the vicar pleaded for decorum. Or had her sectioned.

The radio was still on in the bathroom, David Essex singing that it was only a *Winter's Tale.* To think all those decades ago, Paul's quiet watchfulness and slate grey eyes had reminded her of her pop crush. He'd watched her a lot then, admiringly and occasionally even jealously. How lovely it had felt to be desired, noticed, engaged.

She selected a black kohl pencil and painted three lines fanning from her nose to her cheeks.

'What are you *doing*?'

She started in surprise to find Paul watching

her in the mirror, now wearing New Zealand flag boxers and Christmas socks.

She managed an enigmatic arch of one brow. 'Shapeshifting.'

He arched both brows in return, and Gill felt a distant memory jog of different rules applying at Christmas.

'What *are* those lines on your face?'

'Wrinkles.'

'You know what I mean.'

'They're whiskers,' she admitted, feeling stupid.

'Is tonight fancy dress?'

'No, I just thought...' That you wouldn't notice. Except he had noticed. She heard her voice covering her mistake with its customary gung ho. 'I'd try something different. Bad idea?'

'Bad idea,' he agreed, reaching past her for his antiperspirant. Seconds later, he vanished beneath a white cloud.

Eyes smarting, Gill plucked out a cleansing wipe and started removing the whiskers, realising too late that she was rubbing off the tan hound eye patch too, foundation and kohl blurring together, making her look like Bert from Mary Poppins after a street brawl. She rarely swore, but a run of muttered expletives machine gunned under her breath as she took in how genuinely awful it looked.

The deodorant mist had cleared behind her, Paul watching her reflection again, 'Have you been drinking?'

'Not yet.'

How many unhappy spouses would get drunk and flirt with each other tonight, she wondered? After last year's boozy carol circuit, Petra had confessed to a close call with a notorious village lothario. This year, she'd told Gill that money was on merry widow Auriol Bullock making a play for unmarked husbands.

Nobody will flirt with me, Gill thought as she took in her grey-cheeked, swollen-eyed reflection. Least of all, my husband.

In the bathroom, David Essex was still lamenting his lost love.

In the bedroom, Paul was combing his wet hair and examining his reflection in the mirror over Gill's shoulder.

She attacked her chimney sweep complexion with a fresh wipe, thinking about Aunt Evil kissing Ted Marlborough to make her embittered husband jealous, a ruse that had just driven him away. One more love that failed.

Far better to be honest: 'We have to do something to help our marriage, Paul.'

He flashed a humouring smile. 'Where's all this come from?'

'Don't tell me you haven't felt it, too.'

'Are we really having this conversation now?' Turning away, he picked up his watch to strap it back on, checking the time as he did so. 'We're due on show in twenty minutes.'

In the bathroom, David Essex had given way to

Cerys Matthews and Tom Jones, complaining it was cold outside.

Inside her warm house, icy goose bumps were popping up everywhere as Gill locked eyes with her reflection, Evelyn's words in her head: *Far lonelier being with somebody who acts like you're not there, who doesn't see you, don't you think?*

'Yes, we're having this conversation now, Paul.'

She heard his impatient breath, caught the exaggerated slump of his shoulders in the mirror, and watched him swing around. Then he swore in shock.

'You've got a black eye!'

'I thought that's what it was,' she reached for the orange foundation.

'How the hell – what the – I mean, when did this happen?'

Gill thought about Aunt Evil's regret again, Betty Marlborough's diffidence, Lindy's fierceness, her resolve hardening. 'You remember I told you I was once engaged to a local farmer? Well, his wife punched me this morning. It was just the wake-up call I needed to try to save our marriage.'

That got his attention.

*

As the carollers gathered on the snowy Green, Petra consciously uncoupled from her punk-trousered back end, abandoning Charlie to the mulled wine stall while she crunched across the footprints and snowman-making trails to seek out Mo and Bridge for an emergency Saddle Bags conflab, donkey head under one arm.

'Jesus, that's like some sick laboratory experiment, so it is,' Bridge eyed the hastily adapted cow costume.

'What happened up at the Marlboroughs' farm?' Mo demanded, beckoning the other two behind a horse chestnut for privacy.

Petra debriefed them about Gill's shiner and their hasty getaway. 'I blame myself entirely, but who knew Robbie was such a sleazebag?'

'Oh, I got those vibes straight away in the pub,' Bridge said emphatically. She was wearing novelty light-up reindeer antlers over her fluffy beanie. 'Total sleaze, no bag. Not worthy of bagdom.'

'He was a bit "poor me",' Mo agreed, pink-cheeked in a sequinned Santa hat and snowball ear-warmers.

'The thing is, I think I might have triggered something.'

'Gill would never cheat on Paul!' scoffed Bridge.

'Or leave him,' Mo insisted.

They absorbed this mutual reassurance briefly before sharing the same silent horror.

'What about him?' Bridge voiced it first, never one to hold back on her criticism of the Bardswolds' most uptight, anally retentive vet.

'Paul's a great dad,' Mo reassured her gently. 'He knows his horses, never lets the pub quiz team down, and loves Gill in his way.'

'Still, he's Paul,' Bridge countered. They'd all heard enough on their hacks to know Gill's husband was supremely tricky.

'What have I *done*?' wailed Petra. 'I have to go round there.'

'You can't,' Mo squeaked. 'Your ass is needed here. Look.'

The vicar had arrived to lead the procession in a black cassock so long it was snow-ploughing the Green. But all eyes were on Auriol Bullock, upstaging God's representative in full Angel Gabriel regalia with light-up halo, widespan wings knocking carol singers aside as she twirled round to greet them all, then cried out: 'Here come my flock!'

A small clutch of Compton Magna primary school children was crossing the green in smocks and tea towels, some with lamps on crooks, others tugging a trio of reluctant miniature French sheep that one of the parents kept as pets.

'*Where* is my donkey?' demanded Auriol.

Then everyone turned as a livestock lorry rumbled into the village, colourful lights haloing the cab, its stereo blasting out *Santa Claus Is Coming To Town.*

*

'I am not having any sort of affair, Paul. Will you just *listen*?' Gill wailed, exasperated.

Her husband was still wearing his Kiwi flag pants, Santa chimney socks and an ever-more panic-stricken expression. 'I *am* listening.'

'I went to Robbie's farm because Petra was desperate to borrow a donkey for tonight, and we knew his mother used to keep a herd – which incidentally she named after this family, including you – and it brought it all back, and I think he just got carried away, plus he's terribly like his father and -'

'I do NOT want to hear this!' Paul covered his ears, shouting. 'One minute we're perfectly happy, and the next you're –'

'*HAPPY?*' Gill laughed hollowly. The tears that she so rarely ever let loose were defying her, stripping away the orangey foundation to reveal the full glory of her black eye. 'We are *not* happy. I am not happy. I want to make us happy again.'

The hands lowered slowly from his ears, testing the space to talk. 'I do, too.'

'So why do you keep messaging *her*?'

'Who?'

'Do I need to say her name?'

'Er…yes?'

She did, and he started to laugh. 'Oh, Gill, you found me out –'

'You BASTARD!'

'Oh, DO stop bickering!' The door swung open. 'I'm ready for the carol singing!'

It was Aunt Evil in a vintage astrakhan coat, platform boots and Cossack hat, the family's excited dogs crowding past her. 'Irresistible pants, Peter – Patrick – *Paul* darling, Ralph had some just like it. Please kiss and make up, and can you be quick? I need to be at this carol singing pronto!'

'Not now, Evelyn,' Gill pleaded.

'But I've arranged a lovely surprise!'

'Not now,' Paul backed up his wife.

'*NOW*,' Aunt Evil ordered. 'I have a date.'

*

On the Green, the front and rear ends of the Pantomime donkey had redocked, and the corallers were forming a circle. But the vicar's rousing welcome was being overshadowed by the clattering of small hooves on lorry ramp.

Petra half-passed away from the crowd to get a better view.

'What is going on?' demanded her back end, trying to keep up.

'The Marlborough family have arrived,' the front end told him, watching in astonishment as a small, four-legged tribe was led down a lorry ramp, plunging and side-kicking. 'With about a dozen feral-looking donkeys.'

'I hope none of them are feeling randy,' the back end hugged her closer.

*

Gill's black eye shone brighter than the moon overhead and the snow below as she gripped her aunt's hand on one side, her husband shadowing the other. Livid that their big confessional had been interrupted, Paul was goose-stepping alongside, eyes fixed on her. Gill couldn't look at him, equally mad at herself for not waiting until after the village gathering to address the betrayal. Nineteen-year-old Gill had possessed far more self-control.

It was a short walk from the cottage to the Green, but Evelyn's frailty and footwear made for slow going in the snow.

'I can't believe you still have your old platform boots, Aunt Evil.' Gill was grateful that her Walcote upbringing kept the merry platitudes coming.

Oblivious to all crosscurrents, Evelyn was in her coquettish prime again. 'Oh, I bought these on Asos last week, darling. I'm a convert to fast fashion. There he is! My date!'

Loping across the snow to greet them, Ted Marlborough was scrubbed up in a three-piece tweed suit and trapper hat, leading out a cynical-looking beige-coated donkey. Gill recognised her namesake with a mood-lifting gulp. Her quest had been fulfilled after all.

Then she let out a gasp of astonishment.

Because behind his father, in his long stock coat and bush hat, Robbie was tugging along a brace of wise-eyed oldies; hoody-cool Travis followed with matching sleepy siblings, and there were Gill's daughters juggling the lead ropes of a skittish quartet, including the Betty-faced matriarch and the small, grumpy male that reminded her of Paul. Bringing up the rear, wild-haired and laughing loudly as ever, Lindy Marlborough had a trio of braying little show-offs in white, brown and black, all on springs.

When Ted joined Aunt Evil, he kissed her on both cheeks and handed over the donkey's lead rope, which she passed ceremoniously on to her niece, gripping her hand. 'My Christmas present, Gill darling! Because your horse is lonely. Now he'll have *friends*.'

More lead ropes were soon being pressed on Gill, first by a sheepish-looking Robbie avoiding her eyes, then a sleepy Travis smiling straight into them, next her distracted daughters whispering that this was the best thing ever, and finally fierce-smiling Lindy, who hugged Gill so tight she went tip-toes rigid, lead ropes dropping.

'Like I said on the phone,' Lindy bellowed in her ear, 'I left Bob and Ted to load them all up.' She seized Gill's shoulders and held her at arm's length like a surfboard, waggling her triumphantly before taking her hands and gripping them, Robbie's grandmother's ring glinting on her little finger. 'Look after Paul, will you? He's the only one I like.'

'Me too,' she said in a small voice.

Beside Gill, Paul, the husband, had gathered up all the lead ropes, too shocked to remember to be angry. 'Where do we put all these?'

'We have a field,' Gill said, privately wondering much the same. 'My chap could use the company.'

'But I already bought him a companion for Christmas,' Paul muttered indignantly. 'A horse companion.'

She turned to stare at him wide-eyed.

'Bought *us* one,' he eyed her back warily, 'That's what I was trying to tell you earlier. I wanted to keep it as a surprise.' Their bubbly veterinary nurse was selling her young thoroughbred now that she and her boyfriend were expecting their first baby, he explained. 'They have too many neds with a family to raise.'

114

Nids, Gill smiled, her heart suddenly molten, realising at last what all the secretive phone messages had been about.

'I thought we should maybe ride together again?' he looked at her hopefully, then laughed as Gill let out a cry of delight, which sent several donkeys skittering away.

'Seems I've been out-gifted by for a dozen asses,' he blew out a frustrated breath.

'They're cute, you have to admit.'

'Bloody cute,' he leaned against her, and they admired the dozen donkeys in their hands, then each other.

'They're family now,' Gill told him, secretly thrilled by the prospect of the little elderly herd of long-eared Walcote-Wishes retiring together behind their cottage. And also by the idea of cantering alongside her husband on two tall *nids* again.

'I refuse to be a Saddle Bag,' he warned her in an undertone.

'Not even an honorary one?' She kissed him.

'You can be my bit on the side-saddle bag.' He kissed her back.

'Never! I ride astride and set the pace.'

'Is that a promise?'

'I'll show you later.'

*

The front end of the panto donkey was in shock. 'I think I just saw Gill *snogging* her husband.'

'Who cares?' The back end gripped her hips tighter. 'I have the best view in the world. Are we off?'

'*And* Aunt Evil is kissing Ted Marlborough!'

'Hooray - shall we trot on?'

'That's one of Gill's girls necking gorgeous Travis.'

'Is this an orgy or a carol-singing procession?

'Our son and the other daughter are at it now!'

'Speaking as the demoted donkey end here, I'm not sure your eyes and ears are where our hearts and minds should be, Petra darling. This is a religious gathering.'

'We're not much of a donkey, though, are we? Oh, they're off!'

The Nativity procession was finally moving, jingle bells ringing, sheep bleating and donkeys braying. *We Wish You a Merry Christmas* was being sung in four parts, led by members of Auriol's light operatic society.

'Shall we?' the back end of the cow-donkey fondled the front.

'You know what Coll would do?' The front end pushed back eagerly.

'Go home and pogo to the Sex Pistols?'

'Make my Christmas, Punk.'

*

'They're quite a clan,' Gill warned her gelding, who was nickering and whinnying over his stable door, thrilled at the sight of a dozen small, long-eared neighbours cavorting in the paddock beyond his. 'But you have a new friend coming soon, so you won't feel such a giant, short-lugged weirdo.'

'Reckon they're settled for now,' Paul joined her, breathless from throwing hay bales out for the new arrivals. 'Are they really named after your family?'

'*Our* family,' she corrected. 'And yes.'

'That's a bit weird, isn't it?'

'Not if you knew Betty. They've been waiting to come home, that's all.'

'Gill's my favourite already,' he kissed her.

'You shouldn't have favourites,' she kissed him back. 'Paul's mine.'

As the kiss deepened into something they hadn't shared for a long time, Gill felt the thrill of Christmas rules, praying it would last.

'Let's go to bed,' Paul said when they finally came up for air.

'You go ahead. I'll get the lights.'

'Be quick,' he planted another long kiss that left her lips eager to chase his upstairs, his soft laughter tracing its warmth to her ear. 'Still think it's weird her naming them after us lot.'

As her husband headed back across the snowy yard to the house, Gill lingered for a moment, breathing in the bliss of a snow-covered midwinter's night, before turning to press her cheek against her gelding's long, familiar jaw.

'Merry Christmas, Marley,' she whispered.

*

On the other side of the village, dancing to a shouty, high-speed punk cover version of *All I Want for Christmas Is You* in the Gunns' vast, open-plan reception, Auriol Bullock and the Reverend Jolley agreed that it had been a thoroughly triumphant Nativity procession, despite the snow. Villagers on glowing doorsteps had given generously to the church clock repair find. The Comptons' corallers had been in full voice, the children's descant adding wonderfully to the traditional songs, the animal procession gloriously evocative, even though the donkeys had turned out to be a little disorderly. Uncontrollable even.

'If I was being picky, I do think there were one too many donkeys, do you agree?' Auriol shouted over the music as she did the mashed potato energetically.

'On the contrary,' the Reverend swayed on the spot and projected as if from the pulpit, admiring her vivacious rhythm, 'the Bible contains many of the little fellows. Donkeys symbolise hard work, love and peace, whereas horses signify war, wealth and power.'

'I'm all for love and peace!' Auriol threw in a few overhead claps.

'Rather!' The vicar swayed a bit faster, thinking how lovely it would be to have some love and peace, should He approve.

'Perhaps that's why there was a bit of a 'seventies free love festival vibe this evening?' Auriol pulled a scandalised face as she waggled her elbows, but her eyes glittered. 'So much kissing and not a spring of mistletoe in sight. I hope my little shepherds weren't corrupted.'

'Love makes Our Lord very happy, Mrs Bullock,'

Hilary Jolly gave her a hot look. 'Especially at Christmas.'

They danced closer together, eyes locked.

Shimmying her shoulders seductively, Auriol sensed a long, dry spell coming to an end. The vicar wasn't the only one quietly hoping they might just be about to make their Lord happy with peace and love.

Realising one of the Walcote-Wish daughters was videoing them on her phone, she threw in a quick TikTok routine her Year 5s had taught her. 'Come on, vicar, shake a leg! People will watch this in years to come.'

Springing into action, the vicar did an impressive reverse camel walk around her, fingers clicking. 'Yes, let's show them how much festive fun Compton Magna had in these olden days, Mrs Bullock!'

'Oh, I think we'll have fun for years to come, don't you?' Auriol predicted positively aglow with mutual attraction.

They exchanged another sizzling look before turning to blow kisses and wave at the camera. But their videographer had turned away to film the other guests, old and young, coupled and single, born-and-bred villagers, newcomers and weekenders, some dancing, others chatting, a festive bounty of laughter and novelty jumpers and punky, seasonal goodwill. Then, a cheer went up as the music changed, and they all started singing along to *White Christmas*.

And even though it was the Iggy Pop cover version, not Bing Crosby, his deep voice decadently dissipated and laced with irony, it was perfect. Because the gathered villagers knew nothing could stay the same, and yet when the Comptons were covered with snow, and Christmas was nigh, time didn't seem to matter.

ABOUT THE AUTHOR

Fiona Walker

Fiona Walker is the author of over twenty novels, from tales of flat-shares and clubbing in nineties London to today's romping, rural romances set amid shires, spires and stiles. In a career spanning three decades, she's grown up  alongside her readers, never losing her wickedly well-observed take on life, lust and the British in love.

Fiona lives in Warwickshire, sharing a slice of Shakespeare Country with her partner Sam, their two daughters and a menagerie of animals.

PRAISE FOR AUTHOR

THE COMPTONS SERIES

Escape to the country and fall in love with the Comptons.

Old friendships, new loves, jealousies, gossip and beautiful horses – these are the classic ingredients for Fiona Walker's gripping, sexy series, set in the Cotswold village of Compton Magna and laced with her trademark humour.

The Country Set

They say you should never go back.

But this is exactly what ravishing Ronnie Ledwell does, twenty-five years after she scandalized the Cotswold village of Compton Magna by abandoning husband and children for her lover. But her father's famous stud farm has seen better days. Faithful Lester, the gifted stallion man, has guarded Ronnie's secrets for three decades, but can they both forgive and forget the past? Meanwhile, charismatic Kit

Donne can't stand the sight of the woman who so reminds him of his beloved late wife. Greedily eyeing up the estate is sexy Bay Austen, a man who usually gets what he wants. Can Ronnie stand in his way?

In a village riven with affairs, rivalries and scandals, Ronnie's unexpected return, with all its glamour and mystique, sets in motion a drama from which there will be no turning back.

Country Lovers

Glamorous Ronnie Percy has been back home in the Cotswolds for a year. But not everyone has forgiven her for abandoning her family twenty-five years ago.

Ronnie's daughter Pax is fighting for custody of her small son as her own marriage disintegrates. Now she is furious to have to spend New Year's Eve waiting to meet some stranger, invited by her mother to help run the family stud farm. The staunchly loyal head groom, Lester, is even more annoyed. Does Ronnie think he's lost his touch?

Luca O'Brien, Irish charmer and reputed heart-breaker, is known throughout the countryside as the Horsemaker. But what happened to Luca's beautiful stallion, Beck, now broken and unrideable in the Compton Magna stables? And what is Luca running away from?

Passionate, sexy, gripping, and laced with wicked humour, this is bestselling Fiona Walker at her dazzling best.

Country Secrets

Can you ever have a second chance at first love?

When Ronnie Percy's gorgeous on-off lover Blair is forced to deep-freeze their affair for the sake of his sick wife, she's delighted to be distracted by charismatic neighbour, Kit Donne, and – more surprisingly – finds herself drawn into a fight for the future of the village. But then the return of someone from her distant past threatens to expose long-buried secrets.

Meanwhile daughter Pax – already besieged by her controlling estranged husband – has started to suspect that new beau 'the horsemaker' Luca still loves somebody else. The last shoulder on earth she should cry on is Bay Austen's, but his marriage is crumbling and he's lost none of his dangerous charm. Moreover, Bay knows the way to her heart is through her horses...

Printed in Great Britain
by Amazon